ANGEL

LAURA LEE

DSP PUBLICATIONS

Published by
DSP PUBLICATIONS

5032 Capital Circle SW, Suite 2, PMB# 279, Tallahassee, FL 32305-7886 USA
http://www.dsppublications.com/

Angel
© 2015 Laura Lee.

Cover Art
© 2011 Anne Cain.
annecain.art@gmail.com.
Cover Design
© 2011 Mara McKennen.
Cover content is for illustrative purposes only and any person depicted on the cover is a model.

ISBN: 978-1-63476-173-4
Digital ISBN: 978-1-63476-174-1
Library of Congress Control Number: 2015904659
Second Edition November 2015
First Edition published by Itineris Press, 2011.

Printed in the United States of America
∞
This paper meets the requirements of
ANSI/NISO Z39.48-1992 (Permanence of Paper).

For my father.

Acknowledgments

DEEPEST GRATITUDE to Jennifer Hunter, who was not only *Angel*'s first reader but the most constant supporter of this project. Thank you to Crystal Brunell, Jodi Connors, Lisa Crawford, Carol Lee, Jennifer Lee, and Laura Ross for their generous feedback.

Thank you to my thoughtful editor, Lynn West, whose keen eye for detail helped shape *Angel*, and to cover artist Anne Cain, who gave the concept of an angel a beautiful shape.

THE MOUNTAIN

"From the muses of Helicon, let us begin our singing, that haunt Helicon's great and holy mountain, and dance on their soft feet round the violet-dark spring...."

—Hesiod, "Theogony"

THE MOUNTAIN is nothing but itself. It does not speak. It has no message, and yet it is the great metaphor maker. It reflects what the traveler brings to it: a getaway, quiet majesty, a challenge, security, or danger. It is all these things or none of them, and the traveler sees whichever he looks for in it. For millennia people have come to high mountains and sat at their feet or scaled their peaks, hoping to return with the answer to a question.

Six days a week, from Tuesday through Sunday, Paul Tobit drove a sightseeing bus on the winding roads at the base of Mount Rainier in Washington. People often asked him if he got tired of the view. He never did. The mountain was vast enough to provide endless material for wonder and contemplation. There was the sheer majesty of the towering peak, the way it changed with the seasons and the weather, the sense of danger and foreboding that came with its snow cap, where the oxygen was thin and adventurers risked life and limb for the chance to say they reached the summit.

"Magnificent in its symbiosis." Those were the words Paul usually used on his tours to describe Rainier. Up on the mountain, everything is interconnected. The logs fall and they turn into mulch, which becomes soil for new trees. There's an algae up there that grows in a wispy hanging vine. It somehow draws from the tree without choking it. To Paul, it was evidence of the hand of God.

The philosopher Edmund Burke described two different responses to natural beauty in his treatise *On the Sublime and Beautiful*: one originates in love, the other in fear. Fields full of flowers, meadows and ponds covered in lilies are comforting; they give people a sense of harmony and security. They are pretty, but they are not sublime. To be sublime, a landscape has to evoke not only beauty but terror—a sense of something so great, so enormous, with a life span so long that we can scarcely comprehend it. It renders us weak and insignificant in comparison.

Mount Rainier is sublime. Even the most arrogant man would have to be humbled in its presence. It reminds us that the world is much bigger than we are, that there are still places that we cannot blast, or sell, or pave, or control. Is it any wonder that Jesus, who "went up to the mountain to pray," came down with the message that "the meek shall inherit the earth" and delivered the sermon "on the mount"?

Paul enjoyed his job. There was no gossip, no politics, no deadlines or performance reviews. He found both solitude and company on the side of the mountain. The tourists who filed onto his bus each day were always in a good mood—you don't take a sightseeing tour to be miserable and grumpy. The groups bonded quickly over their shared temporary interest in snapping photos of nature. After a pleasant day together, they parted ways without any messy breakups or accusations.

People take vacation snaps in a futile attempt to capture the mountain and the moment so they can take them home to flat states like Indiana and Kansas. There is something in our DNA that makes us want to hold onto the transitory. Photographs give us the pleasing illusion that we can. Yet the image never quite evokes the experience…. "The picture doesn't do it justice. You had to be there."

People also take photographs so they will not feel lonely. They take them for the absent friends they wish were there to share the view. There are few things more melancholy than looking out on a truly sublime landscape and realizing you are experiencing it all alone. This was something Paul knew quite well.

The ritual of being a tour guide appealed to him. What was for the tourists a singular experience was for Paul a repeating experience. Each day he would unlock the bus, jot notes in a couple of logs, and fill the gas tank. At 10:00 a.m., the visitors started to file in with their passes and take their seats. Some privacy-loving folks went straight for the back. The ones who liked to ask questions sat near the front. In the middle were the social ones who hoped to meet their new neighbors during the ride.

Paul rounded a familiar curve in the road and heard the expected sighs and murmurs as the tourists saw a spectacular view for the first time. He had developed an act of sorts over the course of two years. He knew what guests always asked, and he told them before they had the chance. He knew what jokes and lines made people laugh. He had his share of inspirational and thought-provoking observations too. And if that wasn't the group's mood, he could ply them with trivia and hold a contest, awarding a T-shirt to the winner. At the end of the day, his pocket was always stuffed with more than his share of tips. He would never become rich on his mountain proceeds, of course, but he had everything he needed—regular meals, a small cabin with a spectacular view, and time to gaze at the mountain and reflect on life.

Throughout his tours, Paul liked to make references to burning out on his old job. Inevitably, toward the end of the tour, someone would ask what his old job had been. He loved their reactions when he said, "A minister."

"SPECIAL FRIEND"

"I summited Mount Rainier." Words are inadequate to the experience—all the preparation, every single step, the times you think you can't go on, the cold, the thin air—all that it means to accomplish that feat—it's lost to everyone but the individual who undertakes the journey.

OF ALL the parts of his job as a minister, Paul liked funerals the most. Of course, "like" wasn't the right word. No one "liked" having to perform a funeral. Yet ever since his wife, Sara, died, Paul found funerals, and only funerals, truly satisfying. Though he was an introvert by nature, he had always been a compassionate and thoughtful minister. Even as a young man just starting out in his ministry, he intuitively grasped when to offer comforting words and when to allow a silence. He had a stock of memorial prayers that made people cry and smile with private memories in the right balance. You could say he had developed the craft and had a good funeral technique.

After Sara died, however, Paul felt the full weight of performing funerals. He became part of a fraternity of grief and understood all the emotions of the person in front of him. He remembered the small gestures: the offers of food, the shared memories, the shoulders he cried on. He came to believe he could give sermons for the rest of his life and it would never have as much meaning as holding a recent widow's hand and letting her cry for as long as she needed. It was the one time he still felt blessed to be a minister, to have the opportunity to know he was making a difference.

Until she got sick, Sara had been full of life and energy. It seemed like only yesterday that they had met. She sat behind the reception desk in the church office. He was smitten immediately by her charming freckles, her mane of curly red hair, and her warm and genuine smile. She made it her life's mission to help him take his life less seriously. He never fully understood how someone so personable, outgoing, and universally loved could have chosen him. His joy existed in her. When he buried her in the cemetery beside the church, he buried his joy with her.

Could it really have been six years since Sara died? Sometimes it seemed like an eternity, and sometimes it seemed like only a day. At first he had believed it had to be a mistake. Someone like Sara could not possibly stop existing. She would walk through the door in her favorite pastel dress and laugh the way she always had. It was months before that feeling stopped haunting him.

The constant invasive memories of Sara stopped after the first year. One day he woke up and realized he hadn't thought of her at all the previous day. Then two days passed without thinking of her. Then more. He stopped expecting her to be there. He found ways to take care of himself, to work around her absence, yet he could never truly fill the void she left behind. There was no substitute for the role she had played in his life.

He continued to live mostly on the momentum of his habits. He got up on Tuesday morning (Monday was a minister's day off) and drove to the church with about as much enthusiasm as someone would drive to an office cubicle for a job counting widgets. He met with people about weddings and baptisms and pasted on his best ministerial smile. He sat through the meeting to plan the sermon with Emily, the music director, and Marlee, the religious education director, and let his experience carry him through.

He waited for the mail in the early afternoon, a highlight of his day that inevitably disappointed. (No engraved invitations to lunch with the governor, no handwritten personal letters, just a few advertisements and newsletters from other churches.) Then he went home, heated up a frozen dinner, ate it off a folding table in front of the TV, went to bed around ten, and the whole thing started again.

Today was a Wednesday, normally a complete throwaway of a day, but fortunately, Paul thought, he had a funeral to plan. It made getting out of bed easier. He entered the church through a back hallway that led to the office. It was already unlocked when he arrived, which meant Julie was in.

Julie had assumed the reception duties at the church after Sara became the minister's wife. Now in her midforties, she had blonde hair, which she often wore in a long French braid. She had many of the same qualities that had made Sara perfect for the job. She was patient, warm, and interested in people. She was also the gossip hub of the church. Churches have files and records, but most of the real information about a congregation resides in the receptionist's head. If you wanted to know anything about anyone in the church, it was Julie, not Paul, who could tell you.

Paul stopped in the restroom behind Julie's desk and examined his face in the mirror. At forty-two, his hair was already salt-and-pepper gray. The hair at his temples had gone completely white, and he was starting to thin a bit at the crown. He reached down and grabbed the spare tire around his waist. It didn't quite qualify as a "beer belly," but he was certainly not the trim man he had been twenty years before. That was his real body, of course; this replacement was some kind of mistake. Paul thought the dark circles under his eyes made him look three times his age.

Then he had an even more disquieting thought. Maybe he looked exactly his age. Paul threw some water on his face, then went into his office and waited for his meeting with Stuart Briggs.

When Mary Adams died at age eighty-one, it came as a surprise to no one. The end came after years of slow decline that took her motor skills, memories, and sanity. Then there was the long death watch. She held on, uncomprehending and in pain, for weeks. She finally slipped into a welcome unconsciousness, where she remained for several days before finally letting go. "At least she's not suffering anymore," people usually said.

Through all of it, Stuart Briggs was at Mary's side. Mary was Stuart's first and only love. They had met in high school and hit it off right away, but for whatever reason, Mary never was attracted to him. They never dated. Stuart waited in the background as she dated other boys. He was a guest at her wedding to another man. When her first husband died, Stuart was there, hoping for his chance, but it never came. He waited through a second marriage, which ended in divorce.

After that, Mary came to rely on Stuart's constancy. He was the person she called when she needed someone to go with her to the movies, to help her with an errand, or just to talk. They became regular companions, but as far as anyone could tell, they never had a physical relationship and it was never a romance, at least not for her.

When Mary became ill, it was Stuart who cared for her. He took her to church on Sundays, pushing her in her wheelchair even as walking became a challenge for him. He was calm and patient with her confusion and mood swings. He visited her daily in the nursing home long after she had forgotten his name. He stayed with her every day she was in the hospital and then in hospice. He was there when she died, holding her hand. Now he was making the funeral arrangements because Mary's children were scattered across the country in California and Colorado.

He now sat before Paul holding a small scrap of newsprint. It was Mary's obituary, a short notice mentioning her career as a teacher and her long membership in the church. It named her first husband ("predeceased by….") and said she was survived by her two children and their families. Stuart was identified only as "special friend." He had loved Mary longer than her husband; longer than anybody. The center of his world was gone, and yet he had no official title to acknowledge his status. When someone says, "I lost my wife," everyone understands the magnitude of that loss. "I lost my friend" is different. Unless you know the person well, it has no meaning at all.

As Stuart talked about his thoughts for the service, Paul thought about obituaries. When a person you love dies, the obituary takes on an outsized importance. It is the community record that this person lived; she was here; her life did not pass without notice. Yet obituaries are also almost always flat and disappointing. They consist of a dry list of job titles and accomplishments and official connections. But what about the unofficial connections we have in life? Where are the teachers who changed our whole perspective; the mistresses; the dear, dear friends; the ones who worshiped us with unrequited love? What about the ones who got away? The ones we pined for who never returned our affections? Where do they fit?

Obituaries are written in shorthand, sketching out a biography but leaving out all the context that creates a full life. Marital status is a shorthand, but a misleading one. You can be a devoted spouse or a disinterested spouse, an abusive spouse or a supportive spouse. You might have married for love or social status. It is all marriage. Career titles are a shorthand. The deceased held a job, but was it his main sense of pride and identity, or something he dragged himself to every day to pay the bills? You will never know from a death notice. Even seemingly straightforward words like "mother," "father," "daughter," and "son" are shorthand. Was your brother "like a brother" to you, or were you distant or rivals? Was your father the constant presence who taught you to play baseball and took you to Cub Scouts, or was he the man who had sex with your mother and disappeared? Was your relationship with your mother loving or strained and difficult?

The shorthand of obituaries is meaningful to those already in the know—but then, they don't really need the biography. Our obituaries, our biographies in general, are a show for those who know us the least. Paul thought he had stumbled onto the very definition of what it means to be intimate, to know someone well. It is to understand the meaning of those shorthand words for a particular individual, to understand the ambiguities of a life, the parts that do not fit neatly into boxes.

When he had finished his meeting with Stuart, Paul walked to the cemetery next to the church and sat on the ground beside Sara's stone, on the plot where he hoped his bones would one day be buried. The cemetery was designed to be peaceful and meditative. It was far enough from the road that the cars sounded like a distant breeze.

"Have you seen Mary Adams?" Paul asked Sara's slab of granite. "I'm doing her service this weekend. She's probably with you now." He paused, imagining but not hearing her answer. "Stuart had a picture of her from when she was young. She was pretty. It was like looking at another woman, another time…. You'll never be old, will you?"

He sat for a moment, pulling weeds from the grass by his feet.

"I don't know what's going to happen to him. People are supportive. They're all taking shifts bringing him food. But what is he going to do when they leave? I don't know whether to pity him or admire him. I can't imagine being that committed to anything. There's something noble in it." He sighed.

"God, I miss you, Sara. I just don't know what I'm doing anymore. You had a way of pointing me in the right direction. My job is to inspire people. How can I do that if I'm not inspired? I don't need God to send an angel down on a cloud to touch me on the shoulder. But I wouldn't mind a little spark of inspiration. I just want to wake up to life again, to feel the presence of God in something. I'm just going through the motions, and the members of the church deserve better."

He sat listening to his own thoughts, feeling the absence of Sara's replies, until the ticking of the clock seemed to penetrate the walls, calling him back to his normal state of unproductive busyness. He stood and smiled at the stone as if it could smile back at him. Then he walked through the courtyard and back, he thought, to his normal routine.

ANGEL

"Every angel is terrifying," begins Rainer Maria Rilke's "Second Elegy." "But if the archangel now, perilous, from behind the stars took even one step down toward us: our own heart, beating higher and higher, would beat us to death. Who are you?"

The poet describes angels as "mountain ranges, peaks growing red in the dawn of all Beginning."

PAUL ENTERED the church foyer still lost in his thoughts. While his eyes were adjusting to the dim light (it took longer these days) he was nearly blind. Across from him, the front door opened, and bathed in the rays of the late-morning sun was a startling vision. It was an angel, a radiant, luminous being. Her long hair, like spun gold, surrounded her in a halo. Her huge eyes, the color of the ocean, were a portrait of childlike wonder and love. For a moment, Paul was so moved by his mystical vision he was tempted to fall on his knees right there and pray to God.

He took a step forward and squinted. As the figure came into sharper focus, he realized his mistake. He was not looking at an angel, nor was it even a woman. It was a young man. He appeared to be in his early twenties. His shoulder-length hair was dishwater brown, not spun gold. It hung forward to obscure his face. He had a slim build, not bony, but more "skinny" than "thin." He wore a white long-sleeved T-shirt with a picture of the Pillsbury Doughboy in the center paired with tattered jeans. Paul felt a twinge of embarrassment over his mistake—human for angel, man for woman—but his fascination with the being was not diminished.

The visitor ran his finger beside his ear and tucked the wayward strand of hair behind it, revealing his entire face for the first time. Paul had never seen a face so beautiful outside an art museum. A dimple in the chin and the slightest trace of stubble made his jawline masculine. That and his strong cheekbones contradicted the delicate, feminine nature of the rest of his features—the upturned nose and soft lips that curled up at the ends, creating a captivating pout. He had a swan-like neck, and his large eyes—were they blue or green?—were as riveting as they had been when Paul thought they belonged to an angel. Each feature was perfection, and the whole was more than the sum of its parts. He was not at all feminine in his movements. Masculine, and yet too pretty to read entirely as a man.

Paul felt his eyes widen as his pupils dilated. His heart began to race. Could the young man hear it from where he was standing? Who on earth was he? Paul was struck with the desire to take up painting just to try to capture his classical beauty. An angel. An angel had walked in through the door of the church. He was simply the most beautiful work of art Paul had ever seen. He was captivated and terrified by the intensity of the feeling.

"Can I help you? I'm Paul, I'm the minister here," he said over the sound of his beating heart. He put out his hand.

The young man took it. The corners of his lips turned up into a curlicue smile. Soft hands. A firm handshake. He was a corporeal being after all. "Hi," he said. "I'm looking for the AA meeting."

The AA meeting. Well, it wasn't exactly what Paul had expected an angel to utter. The young man was not looking for a church or a minister. He would go to his meeting and walk out the door and might never appear again. Normally, Paul would have pointed down the hall and said, "Turn left." Instead, he said, "This way," and he gestured for the younger man to follow.

"Thank you," the visitor said, and he smiled again. It was just a typical everyday smile, the kind you'd give to the clerk at the drug store when she handed you your change. One of his front teeth, the third to the left, was slightly crooked, creating a small gap. Paul seized on the imperfection. The young man had flaws. He could need somebody. He could need a minister.

As hard as he tried, Paul could not come up with anything else to say on that walk of a hundred feet.

"Here it is."

"Thank you," the visitor said with a small nod, and then he started into the room.

Paul called after him, "If you need anything else, let me know."

But he was already taking a seat in the circle of recovering alcoholics. Why had Paul said that? *"If you need anything else?"* He only needed directions. Who wanted lots of personal focus showing up for their AA meeting?

"What am I thinking? He's a man. A man." But he knew it was already too late. The vision had been too powerful. It would not leave him.

It was only the second time in his life that Paul had experienced something he truly believed was a direct message from God. The first had not been nearly as intense. When he was a young man, about the age of the mystery visitor, Paul had prayed for guidance about his career. He asked the Lord if he should become a minister or perhaps study business or law. That night he had a vivid dream in which he met Jesus Christ and kissed his hand. He knew immediately upon waking what he was meant to do with his life. He never doubted God had spoken to him through the dream. For years, Paul prayed to God to give him another sign. He longed for a truly transcendent experience, but he never had another dream or vision. Not until now. Paul had no doubt his vision of an angel was a message of some kind, but this time he had no idea what the meaning was.

He went back to his office and tried to think about the eulogy for Mary Adams. He couldn't. He tapped his pen on the desk and gazed out the window. Wasn't this guy young to already be in AA? He could help this young man, he thought. He could be his mentor and teacher. There was nothing strange about wanting to help someone. That was all it was, surely. God had given him a sign that this was someone he should notice so he could help him spiritually. Yet Paul sensed his attraction went beyond a desire to be of service. What was it?

It wasn't sexual, he told himself. It couldn't be sexual. He was not gay. He had to be feeling something else. Inspiration, a pure appreciation of beauty. There was nothing wrong with admiring beauty where it existed, even in a male form. God had created it. It was divine energy. The guy needed a community, a church home. There was a reason God had sent him through that door right when Paul happened to be standing there. He felt the enormity of fate in the chance meeting. He could not let the young man walk out as though nothing had happened. Somehow he had to find a way to speak to the angel again. He needed to know what these feelings were calling him to do.

He tapped his pen on the desk. The more he waited, the less time passed. How long did AA meetings run, anyway? He left his office and went to Julie's desk, where they kept the three-ring binder that showed how long each room was in use.

"Do you know when the pavilion will be available?"

"Well, there's an AA meeting in there now. Did you need it for something?"

"No. No. Not right now. How long are they in there for?"

"They have the room for an hour and a half."

"That's how long the meeting goes?"

"I don't know. I think they clean up after. Why?"

"Just wondering. I'm going to take a walk in the courtyard to work on my eulogy, if anyone needs me."

He picked up a prayer book and paced into the courtyard. He held the book in front of his face, but the words just danced. He sat down on a bench. From there he could peer over the top of the book and glance into the pavilion window. He knew where the young man was seated and could just barely make out his left side. He was slumped forward with his elbow on his knee. His long hair brushed his shoulder whenever he tilted his head.

Paul suddenly felt uncomfortable spying on an Alcoholics Anonymous meeting, so he tucked the prayer book into his pocket and went back into the foyer. He looked at the bulletin board and took down three out-of-date announcements. Then he straightened the pamphlets in the visitors' rack. That didn't take much time, so he decided to take them all off the rack and arrange them alphabetically by title. Some of the booklets had pictures but no text on the covers. He decided to place those at the end of the rack. Because it was "Hope Church," there were entirely too many *H*s. He hadn't left enough space. He took the pamphlets from last part of the alphabet down on a nearby table. He placed a stack of "Welcome to Hope Church" on the rack and turned around to grab "What Would Jesus Do?" and crashed straight into someone, regaining his balance by placing his hands on the other person's upper arms. It was his angel. They stood with their faces just inches apart. Paul gasped and backed into the rack, causing several copies of "Membership and You" to rain down on the floor.

"Sorry," the young man said. "I didn't mean to startle you."

"It's…. I wasn't looking."

"Well, I was just going to say thanks again for the directions." He turned away and started to walk toward the door.

"Wait!" Paul called after him.

The angel turned back. He raised his eyebrows and tilted his head. Paul had asked him to wait, and he was waiting. The problem was, Paul hadn't planned anything to say beyond that one word.

"Here," he said, handing the young man a pamphlet. "It gives our service hours. You're welcome to come on Sunday. We have a very nice… a very supportive community. You'd like it."

"Yeah, sure. Thanks," he said as he folded the pamphlet and put it in his back pocket. Then he turned and walked away.

That night Paul lay awake in his bed, fascinated and troubled by his vision and embarrassed by his awkwardness around the young man. He replayed every moment, the angel stepping forward and becoming a man, the way he looked when his face was fully revealed, the surprising affection Paul felt on discovering the small gap in his teeth, the warmth from his body when they crashed by the literature rack. He tried to convince himself that his appreciation for the young man's beauty was purely aesthetic. He wanted to gaze on the face again the way he appreciated the beauty of other forms of nature—an expansive canyon or a sunset over the mountains. But human beauty was different. A scenic vista created appreciation and wonder, but not longing. For the stranger, Paul felt longing. Some part of him ached to be in his presence again. He knew, as well, that simply being near him, seeing him, would not be enough. Seeing him again could only increase the longing.

In the privacy of his room, he allowed his mind to explore the nature of this ache. He stopped trying to critique and explain. He came back to the moment when their bodies touched, when their faces were so close, his hands on the visitor's arms. He imagined their lips coming together, his hands exploring the other man's chest. He imagined at first something ethereal—the pair bathed in white light, communing with an angel. But his musings gave way to something much more physical and sweaty, a pure masturbatory fantasy of limbs and tongues and powerful erections.

As he lay in the glow of his climax, he wondered who he was and what this all meant. He thought back to his youth and the forbidden *Playboy* and *Penthouse* magazines he had kept hidden in the crawl space. He remembered the time one of his teachers bent a little too far down and accidentally exposed her right breast, and how that image played into his fantasy life for years; how all-consuming his high school infatuation with Sally Guthrie had been, how nervous he had been about that first kiss and how much persuasion it had taken to get her to third base.

He thought about Sara, how lovely her shyness about her body was. How much he had longed to ravish the paragon of Christian community, to become the only one to unravel her secrets. He loved the freckles that dotted her skin (and that she hated so much), her little teacup breasts (she called herself an "ironing board"), and the undeniable intrigue of the ginger hair that decorated her nakedness. These had not been substitute fantasies. He had not desired women because he thought he was supposed to. The attractions had been as real as the wind and the tides, a true force of nature. So what was this? What *was* this?

The following Sunday, Paul surprised the greeters by joining them in the foyer. He said he'd decided it was much more welcoming if the minister took the time to greet all the newcomers personally. His eyes were wide, and he watched each person coming through the door with a sense of anticipation. The young man never arrived.

"It was nice to see you out there greeting like that," Julie said after the service. "It was a good idea. A lot of people had good things to say about it. Since Sara died, well, it's just nice to see you so engaged again. Like old times."

He greeted the visitors again the following Sunday, and the two after that, and each time he held onto the nervous expectation that his angel would appear. He never did. Each Wednesday afternoon Paul found something to do in the pavilion or the lobby. He watched the alcoholics file in and leave. The visitor was not among them. On every occasion, Paul was both disappointed and slightly relieved. He started to wonder if he had imagined the whole thing. Perhaps the young man did not exist at all.

HERE IS THE CHURCH,
HERE IS THE STEEPLE

Archaeologists think they know what ancient people believed. Ancient tall things were supposed to be monuments to the divine and our modern structures monuments to mankind. We've become self-centered and arrogant. That's what they say. But is that true? The Egyptian pyramids were tombs of the notable people of their day. We inscribe our large buildings with Masonic cornerstones and mythic symbolism. Future archaeologists might think the Sears Tower was built to take us closer to God.

If man was created in God's image and God makes mountains, isn't it natural we'd try to build mountains of our own? Weren't all these structures created out of the same human desire to climb? Building a cathedral is building a mountain. It is the creation of an edifice so large and grand that we are humbled in its presence. Could it be that, paradoxically, the magnificent churches with grand steeples represent a Christianity of humility, not hubris?

PAUL WAS gazing out the conference room window into the foyer and the spot where he had first seen the young stranger. He pictured himself reaching out to him, touching his cheek.

"I'm not saying we shouldn't fix it. I'm just saying it shouldn't be our priority."

Paul's attention snapped back to the room. Mike Davis, the church board president, was serious and pragmatic. Mike was always the alpha in any meeting. He was a business owner who had focused so much of his time and attention on his industry that he couldn't quite keep his focus on a wife. He was now on his third.

As with most churches, the church board was made up entirely of volunteers. They almost always ran unopposed, so the main qualification was a willingness to do the job. The church didn't have to pay them, but that also meant no one could fire them. It was always hard to give people enough appreciation to keep them interested. The rotating boards changed the tone of the administration every couple of years. Sometimes there would be a volunteer who couldn't get around to doing any work but who didn't want to relinquish the title and the position, and everything would grind to a standstill. Other times an overly enthusiastic volunteer would put in so much time and energy that she would start to feel resentful, and she'd end up quitting the church entirely.

Mike brought a serious business tone to the board. He believed strongly that the principles of corporations should be applied to the church. Under his leadership, the board had created a mission statement and posted it everywhere. Their priority was "growth," which they equated with success. Paul had nothing against growth, per se. It would be good for his ego, certainly, to see the pews full each Sunday. But he was uncomfortable with the implication that worship was a product to be marketed the same way you'd sell a soft drink or a pair of designer jeans. It seemed the entire culture had become permeated with a marketplace mentality, and church should be the exception.

Once people had viewed commerce through the lens of faith. Now it seemed people viewed faith through the lens of commerce. Instead of arranging their lives to live in accordance with their faith, they went "church shopping" to find a faith that fit their lifestyle. Something had been lost, Paul believed, yet he realized there was really no way to turn back the clock.

Mike had stirred up so much enthusiasm for his growth mission that it would have been foolish of Paul to try to squelch it. He certainly did not question Mike's intentions or his devotion to the church. Yet the board president was unyielding in his opinions, and it was hard to convince him of the value of anything that could not be quantified. At issue today was the crumbling church steeple, which had become an eyesore and a home for bats. Repairing it properly would cost $30,000, and Mike was in favor of tearing the old thing down.

"People don't choose a church because of what the building looks like," Mike said. "They're not attracted by steeples. They come because they see ads or billboards. What is important is what is inside. The church could be in an old car lot. Advertising is where we need to spend our money if we want to grow."

Paul was having a hard time articulating his argument. He had not received a formal education in the finer points of church architecture and design. He only knew that there *were* sacred places, and they spoke a language he understood without words, beyond intellect. There were places that invited contemplation and places that called for activity and involvement. The mega churches with their rock music, headset microphones, and video screens were as far from his sense of a sacred place as the mind could travel. A church should be a departure from the outside world of constant distraction and stimulation, not an imitation of it.

The little white wooden churches with their towering steeples were created for simple people. Farmers, laborers, and artisans could enjoy a humbler version of the impressive medieval structures that were artists' visions of what heaven might look like. The arched doorway and triangular roof pointed to heaven and also represented the three sides of the trinity. Two spaces off the sides of the sanctuary jutted out and created a cross shape. When a worshiper took communion, he walked through the nave and approached the altar up three steps—the number three again, the trinity. Behind the altar, a high vaulted arch represented heaven. All the time they were surrounded by the cross, metaphorically demonstrating that the path to heaven was through Christ's sacrifice, his death and rebirth.

"There is an entire symbolic language in church design," Paul said. "If you destroy part of the design, you're changing the language. If you take one word out of a sentence, it changes the whole meaning."

"Come on, Paul," Mike said. "It doesn't stop being a church if it has no steeple. The steeple is nice, but it's not necessary."

"No, it's not necessary. But that doesn't mean it's not important."

Paul knew there was a value in architecture, in arts, in beautiful things. Why did those things matter? Because they did. The only way to make a convincing argument for architecture was with poetry, and people who didn't care for art were immune to poetic language as well. You either understood it in your soul or you didn't. Trying to explain the value of aesthetics to Mike was like trying to explain the color blue to someone who'd been blind from birth.

Paul had brought along an illustrated art book, hoping he would find something in it to help make the point that the steeple was worth saving and should be a priority. He flipped through pages of classical devotional art to find an image to demonstrate the clear connection between aesthetics and worship. As he turned the pages, he came upon a reproduction of *Portrait of a Young Woman in Profile* by Sandro Botticelli.

He stopped flipping. He recognized that face. It was his angel. It was not an exact copy, but the resemblance was striking. He ran his finger along the profile, the familiar line of her nose, the curl of her lips. Was it possible he had seen an actual muse? Had this being traveled through time, taking on different forms, inspiring great works of art as she went? No, that was ridiculous. He had shaken hands with a flesh-and-blood man.

"I don't think we're going to make any more progress on this issue today," Mike said. "Let's plan a date for our next meeting."

The meeting ended without a final resolution on the steeple. The general consensus seemed to be that the first priority was growth, that growth would bring in new pledges, and that when the pledges increased, they could discuss fixing the steeple. If they didn't grow enough, fast enough, to increase their income before the steeple rotted away, it would have to come down. Paul vowed to himself that he would write a sermon, or a series of sermons if need be, on the value of beauty in worship, the grand tradition of the old cathedrals, the metaphors built into church architecture, the sacred value of places, the "angels in the architecture," as designers sometimes say. He hoped he could summon enough inspiration to be persuasive.

He went back to his office, shut the door, and stared at the Botticelli painting. Paul thought maybe he understood what he had responded to when he confused the young man for an angel. His face reflected the great works of classical art. It was an archetype for an ideal of beauty that was neither masculine nor feminine. There was nothing obscene about recognizing archetypal beauty when he saw it. He had only confused a sense of recognition for a feeling of desire.

Thanks to advertising and marketing, beauty, in our culture, is almost always linked to desire. A beautiful woman is draped across a new car. Models in bikinis sell beer. You are supposed to want to possess the beauties on television or to be like them. Beauty is a call to action—you're supposed to *do* something when you see it. To just stand back and appreciate it—we don't have time for it anymore. Museums are not interactive enough. We want our beauty to give back. If it doesn't we have no use for it.

Paul's appreciation for the young man was of a different sort. It was elevated and pure, like a trip to the museum. You do not have to be gay to appreciate Michelangelo's *David*. You do not look at a portrait of a reclining nude in a museum in the same way you look at a photo in *Playboy*. Paul wondered if he was feeling the same emotions that Botticelli had felt when he saw his muse.

Paul nearly managed to convince himself that he had only felt attraction to the young man because he loved the woman in the painting. After all, he had confused him for a woman when he walked through the door. The thought comforted him. But for this theory to be true, he would have to have loved the painting before he loved the man. That wasn't the order of things. He did not dream of the stranger because of a resemblance to the artist's model. He stared at the artist's model because she reminded him of the young man. As he gazed at the painting, he tried to edit out her female-ness, to ignore the lavish braids and the heavy red gown and to focus on the features that most reminded him of the man he had seen and so desperately wanted to see again. Paul tore the page out of the book: an uncharacteristic act for someone who had always disapproved of people who damaged books with underlines and margin notes. He pinned the portrait to his bulletin board so he could draw inspiration from it every day.

By night, the inspiration was a different sort. He couldn't resist the urge to imagine himself kissing those soft lips, putting his hands on the angel's narrow hips, drawing him toward his own body. When he gave himself over to the fantasy, it felt wonderful. But the next day, having crossed over into desire for the man and not the image, he was filled with guilt, sadness, and a preemptive sense of loss.

His guilt was not because it was a homosexual fantasy. Over the years, his mind had conjured all kinds of strange and exotic sexual fantasies. Many things that made his toes curl in the confines of his own mind were not things he would ever try in reality, nor did he want to. His guilt was over his failure to love purely, without the desire to possess. He was debasing the spiritual significance of the encounter, transforming it from art to pornography.

Desire could only lead to disappointment. He wanted something down to his bone marrow that he knew could never be. The young man was remarkably attractive. Anyone could see that. He had to be married or surrounded by beautiful women—or both. Even if there was a chance that he could love a man, there was no chance that he would be attracted to an average-looking, forty-two-year-old minister. Each night the fantasy brought Paul soaring to new heights and then brought him crashing down to new depths of loneliness, and the cycle began again.

IAN

The Seattle-based author Bruce Barcott was drawn to Rainier and compelled to climb. "We come for the pretty sights," he wrote, "but also to find a place still free from... life-saving constraints. We come to the mountain seeking beauty and terror."

PAUL WAS determined to write a sermon that would convince everyone of the symbolic value of the steeple. The theme would be great art, classic artists, how they experienced the transcendent and tried to translate that into church architecture for the rest of us poor slobs. He told Julie not to interrupt him. He just needed two good hours to get the sermon written. He went into the office, sat down at his desk, and stared at the computer screen. *So, beauty and Christianity. The spiritual value of recognizing beauty.* He gazed at the portrait on his wall. The words did not come.

Maybe he'd just check his e-mail first. Mike Davis was hyperventilating about attendance again and not reaching their goals for growth—as though they were selling stock in salvation and needed to get a better return on the investment. Mike might not have intended it, but Paul always felt there was an inherent criticism in his messages. There would be more people at the church if only Paul were a better minister, more exciting, more inspiring a little more interesting than Sunday-morning reruns of reality TV programs. Maybe that was his own sense of guilt. He knew he was uninspired these days. The ministry was supposed to be a "calling." Why did it so often feel like a job?

When he had decided to go to theological school, he was full of ideas, the love of Christ, a desire to serve God and make the world a better place. He had never dreamed of budgets, office politics, and dealing with difficult and demanding personalities. There was so much more paperwork than he'd ever imagined. But then again, did anyone really dream about paperwork when they were a kid? Did anyone sit with the guidance counselor and discuss the everyday tasks of the careers they'd chosen? Firemen and airline pilots were probably overwhelmed with paperwork too.

It just seemed like all the nonsense pushed out the time and mental energy for the important things. He could be more present for people in need, and be more inspiring with his sermons, if he wasn't spending so much time going to budget meetings and making decisions about whether to buy or lease a photocopier for the office.

Right. So, a sermon. He picked up the red-letter Bible and thumbed through it. He just needed to find one verse to latch onto, to use as his central metaphor and theme. Nothing was jumping out at him…. Maybe he should speak about e-mail…. Julie was not going to let anyone bug him, and yet here he was clicking on the little envelope icon over and over and being distracted without any help from anyone.

A church member wanted to come in for a meeting to talk about her money problems. She said she felt overworked, tired, and not able to do what she really wanted in life.

Join the club, he thought.

He wrote: "I'm sorry things are so difficult for you now. I have time on Friday at 2:30 if you are free."

It was easy to say the right thing to people most of the time, because they had such ordinary problems. They felt unique to the person experiencing them, but if they'd been in the position to hear everyone else's innermost fears, they would see how commonplace it all was.

But only occasionally there are brief, transcendent moments where everything seems to stop; all the energy of the world falls into harmony. We're transported beyond normal experience and feel the presence of God. You go through the rest of your life powered by those tiny glimpses of the divine.

His mind was invaded once again by the thought of his angel— the way his hair fell onto his face. The way he moved when he walked, his head high, leading with his hips. The absolute perfection of his face. How shaking his hand made Paul feel as though all the atoms in his body had aligned. It wasn't lust, he told himself yet again. It wasn't about sex. It was transcendent. It was spiritual.

The transcendent power of beauty. Moments of appreciating beauty. What did the Bible say about that? Most of the passages he managed to find did not have much to say about the appreciation of beauty.

"Your heart was proud because of your beauty; you corrupted your wisdom for the sake of your splendor." Ezekiel 28:17

"Do not let your adorning be external." 1 Peter 3:3.

If he wanted to write about the dangers of being seduced by beauty, there was a lot of material there. People must need more reassurance that beauty doesn't matter than reinforcement that it does. The transcendent power of beauty—deep aesthetic appreciation—surely the Bible had something good to say about that?

The Song of Solomon seemed promising. Ah-ha! "Behold, you are beautiful, my love, behold, you are beautiful!" Good start. But then it went on: "Your eyes are doves behind your veil. Your hair is like a flock of goats leaping down the slopes of Gilead. Your teeth are like a flock of shorn ewes that have come up from the washing." Teeth like shorn ewes? *Quite right. Powerful beauty makes us talk like idiots. Now there's a promising theme.*

Forget Solomon. Forget beauty. New topic. He gazed out the window.

Why was this so difficult? He remembered how it had been when he was young and full of love for Christ. He was full of passion and wanted to tell everyone the Good News. He had had no problem speaking on any topic and bringing it back to Christ's love. It had flowed out of him naturally. But he had been so arrogant. He had felt as though being faithful made him different. As if he had discovered Christ himself. "He died for *my* sins." But then the arrogance of youth was completely ordinary too.

So how could he write that? How could he make people leave the church feeling uplifted with a message of being not special, but ordinary? He thought he just might have come up with the right lines to build the sermon around when Julie knocked softly and poked her head around the door. "Paul?" The thought disappeared like the traces of a dream when the alarm goes off in the morning.

"I thought I told you not to interrupt me!" He felt bad about snapping at her as soon as he said it.

"I'm sorry," she said, "but we have a problem. I was about to go home and I noticed that there's a man sitting in the pavilion, and I think he's drunk. I was afraid to go up to him."

Paul was actually relieved to have something besides the sermon to focus on. "Okay," he said, "I'll take care of it."

Confrontation had never been his strong suit. He hoped he was not about to encounter a violent drunk. He took a deep breath. As he walked to the pavilion, he practiced his firm but gentle speech in his head: "You can't stay here. There are some places you can go…."

By the time he got to the room, he was mentally prepared for a tattooed biker with scars on his face, shouting, swearing, throwing bottles. He was ready for anything, he thought. Anything but this: a slim figure sitting quietly on the floor, his right side lit by the warm orange rays of late afternoon sun, his arms folded loosely around his knees. His head was down, and his hair fell down around his face, completely obscuring it. But there was no doubt. It was his angel. Paul felt his heart skip a beat.

He sat down beside the young man, close enough to smell whiskey and cigarettes. He spoke softly. "Hi."

The young man turned to Paul and squinted for a moment to focus. Even with a furrowed brow and a face full of confusion, he was spectacularly beautiful.

"What's your name?" Paul asked.

"Ian Finnerty."

Ian. His name was Ian.

Paul was filled with a desire to take him into his arms, hold him, and protect him from all the evils in the world. He settled instead on resting a single hand on Ian's shoulder. "My name is Paul…. Are you okay?"

"I'm just waiting."

"Waiting for what?"

"The meeting."

"What meeting?"

"AA."

"There's no meeting today."

"What?" He looked around the room, checking to be sure he was where he thought he was. "No, it's here. In the church. I remember."

"They come on Wednesday. It's Thursday today."

"It's Thursday?"

"Thursday."

Ian rubbed the back of his neck. "Thursday. Oh."

"Maybe… maybe I can help you. If you need to talk."

"No, I'm fine. It was really just an idea." He put a hand on Paul's shoulder to raise himself to his feet. He stumbled.

Paul stood, then offered Ian a hand to help him up. It took Ian a moment to find his balance. Then he reached into his pocket and produced a set of car keys.

"Wait," Paul said. "You drove here?"

"No. I came off the wagon." As Ian laughed at his own joke, a small tear escaped from the corner of his eye. "There was a wagon, and I came off of it."

"You're too drunk to drive."

"I'm fine."

"Ian," he said with his practiced firm voice, "you're too drunk to drive. I'm going to take you home, and tomorrow you can call me and we'll come get your car. Okay?"

"Yeah, okay." Ian started walking slowly and deliberately. It was a miracle he'd made it to the church in one piece.

Paul believed he understood now. His visions weren't about an artistic appreciation of beauty after all. God had sent Ian to his church in angelic form so that Paul could help him turn his life around. God had let him see his true angelic nature. Paul had simply confused the profound feelings for something more base and common.

As Paul drove, Ian played with the loose threads around a frayed spot in his jeans. They were the kind of jeans that kids bought pretattered for effect. He was very young.

"You ever think about that expression 'on the wagon'?" Ian asked. "They never tell you where the wagon is going. Why should you just jump on a wagon if you don't know where it's going?"

"You may not know where the wagon is going, but you know what it's like where you are now," Paul said. "That's probably why you get on."

"It's got to be better, right?" Ian turned and looked out the window.

"How old are you, Ian?"

"Twenty-four."

Twenty-four. If his life had been a bit different, Paul could conceivably have a son Ian's age. He would have been a young father, just eighteen, but it was certainly within the realm of possibility. He had friends with children almost that old.

"Why were you drinking today?" Paul asked.

Ian turned to Paul and squinted, as though he were thinking about it. He finally answered, "Do I need a reason?"

"You must want to stop. That's why you were here today."

Ian went back to playing with the threads on his jeans.

"My dad was an alcoholic too," Ian said. "'Worthless drunk.' That's what my mom called him."

"Was he abusive?"

"I don't know. He left when I was three."

"I'm sorry."

"I'm probably better off," he said, laughing. "I mean, look how great I've turned out."

"I don't know you well, but I can tell you're smart and—" He stopped himself from saying "beautiful." "You have a lot going for you."

Ian smiled wistfully.

"Do you have a church?" Paul asked. "You could come on Sunday. I'd like it if you did."

Ian turned again and looked back out the window. "Church and I, we're kind of divorced," he said. "Turn left here."

Ian lived on an alley off the town's main street in a run-down apartment building with large stone steps. It looked like a cold concrete block. Nothing about it said "home." It was a dwelling.

Paul took the car's service manual out of the pocket in the door and tore out a blank page. He took a pen out of the cup holder and wrote down his cell phone number and the name "Paul."

"This is my number," he said, handing the paper to Ian. "Call me tomorrow when you're ready to go get your car. Okay?"

"Yeah," Ian said. He took the paper, folded it, and stuffed it into his front jeans pocket. Then he opened the door and stumbled out of the car.

"Do you need me to help you get in?" Paul asked.

"No. I still know how to turn doorknobs," he said.

Paul sat at the curb and watched Ian weave his way up the steps, fumble with his keys in the lock, and then disappear through the door.

On the drive home, Paul reviewed every word of their conversation. He cataloged the information—Ian was twenty-four. He had never known his alcoholic father. He must have felt some connection to Paul to reveal something that personal, right?

"Church and I, we're kind of divorced...."

Paul wondered if he'd made a mistake pushing church. He didn't want Ian to think he was only interested in drumming up attendance at his services. But if Ian didn't come to the church, when would he ever see him again? At least he knew he would have one more opportunity to talk to him when he picked him up. What could he say?

DESECRATION

*The English theologian Thomas Burnet, in spite of a complete
lack of training in science and geography, published a book in the
seventeenth century called* Sacred Theory of the Earth, *which sought to
explain how the Earth came to be the way it is today. He speculated
that up until Noah's flood, the world had been a hollow sphere with the
water inside. When man's sinfulness became too much for God to bear,
he unleashed the water to wash the wickedness away. Mountains
remain as scars on the earth, reminders of a great punishment for our
weakness.*

IT SEEMED quite possible that Paul would not have a sermon at all that
Sunday. He sat at his desk, unable to concentrate on anything but the cell
phone, which he had placed in the center of his desk. He had no intention
of missing Ian's call when it came. His right leg bounced as he checked
his e-mail and pretended not to be waiting for the phone to ring.

It was one thirty before the generic ringtone started to play. Paul
was so startled he nearly jumped out of his chair.

"Hello."

"Hi, um, is this… Paul?"

"Yes. This is Paul."

"Hi, um, this is Ian. I… I think you might have brought me
home? I had your number in my pocket."

"Yes. Are you ready for me to take you back to your car?"

"Yes, please. Thank you."

"I'll be right there."

Ian was sitting out on the front step of his apartment, smoking a
cigarette, when Paul drove up. When he saw the car, he dropped the
cigarette and crushed it out with his foot as he stood up. *Great, his
angel was a smoker too.* Paul had expected to find Ian looking
hungover, sick and pale, but there was no evidence at all of the night
before on his face. His hair was pulled back neatly with a black hair
band. This accentuated his cheekbones and made his eyes seem even

brighter and more alert. He wore plaid slacks, a matching jacket, and a T-shirt with the name of a rock band Paul had never heard of. He looked fashionable, fit and young. When Ian spotted Paul, he was taken aback.

"Wait, you're that minister," he said. "With the pamphlets."

"You seem surprised."

"It's just not what I was expecting." His expression was mischievous, conspiratorial. "So *you* go to the clubs?"

It took Paul a moment to understand, but it finally dawned on him: Ian didn't remember a thing. He'd blacked out the entire previous afternoon and evening. When he found a piece of paper in his pocket with a cell phone number and the name "Paul," he assumed the minister "brought him home." What was this club he imagined he'd been to?

"No," Paul said, a bit defensively. "No. You don't remember yesterday at all?"

Ian scratched the back of his head. "I'm sorry," he said. "It's embarrassing. Sometimes I have these blackouts. But look, if something happened between us, I'm sure...."

"Nothing *happened* between us," Paul snapped. "I'm not.... We had a whole conversation."

Paul had spent every minute since their last meeting replaying every word of the conversation, turning it over for mistakes and clues and meanings, yet for Ian, it had never happened. How could he have erased something so significant to Paul and replaced it with something so impersonal, ordinary, and base?

Ian gazed downward. He looked confused and vulnerable, and it triggered Paul's protective instincts. The more lost Ian looked, the more beautiful he became. And the more beautiful he grew, the more frustrated Paul became. God had created this man with a quick wit and the face of an angel. How could he so easily throw a gift like that away? It was spitting in God's face.

"I'm sorry, I don't remember," Ian said to his shoes.

Paul's tone was harsh. "You were sitting, drunk, on the floor in my church. You showed up on the wrong day looking for an AA meeting that didn't exist. You could hardly walk, and you were going to drive yourself home. So I brought you here to keep you from killing yourself. That's what happened."

"Oh." The blood rushed into Ian's cheeks. "So this would be one of those embarrassing moments."

"Which part? Being falling-down drunk in a church, or confusing the minister for someone you picked up in a gay bar?"

"Yeah" was all Ian had to say.

Paul regretted his harshness. "Come on," he said more gently. "Get in. I'll take you to your car."

They rode for a few blocks in silence. Eventually Ian said, "I'm sorry, you know. I just assumed. It's nothing to do with you. It's just the way my life has been lately."

"It's none of my business, but…."

"But?"

"How often does that happen? You wake up, and you don't know who took you home or what happened the night before?"

"Not very often. A few times. You know, sometimes. It's just the kinds of places I go, if someone takes you home, you figure…. I didn't mean to imply anything. I'm sure you're a good minister."

"It's okay." Paul smiled. "I guess I should be flattered, really. An old guy like me."

Ian relaxed. "You're not that old," he said. "Anyway, I like older men."

The phrase "I like older men" hung in the air. Paul had never spoken openly to a gay man before. He'd never heard a man tell him about his attraction for a certain type of male. It felt wrong. Paul's own aversion confused him. He had been thinking about Ian for weeks, constantly, intrusively. He could recall every contour of his face, the way the corners of his lips curled up when he smiled, his big aqua eyes, the curve of his upturned nose, even the mostly faded chicken pox scar over his left eyebrow and the small mole directly under the center of his right eye—the tiny brown dot was so symmetrically placed that it seemed like the subtle signature of the artist, the autograph of God. He had been unable to stop the sexual fantasies and dreams. Ian was attracted to men. There was at least a chance for the two of them (though Ian was clearly out of his league). This should have thrilled Paul. Why was he upset?

It wasn't entirely jealousy, although that was part of it. The image of his angel being pawed by some clumsy drunken middle-aged man in a dark corner of a bar was almost too much for Paul to bear. The thought that there might have been many, too many to remember, was even worse. It was desecration, pure and simple. It discouraged him about the nature of humanity. Were people all so focused on their own desires that they failed to recognize the gift of divine beauty and to treat it as sacred?

But was the nature of his own desire any different? Was it also a desecration? Or could our basest instincts be purified by love? Only disembodied angels could have a true union of souls. As ridiculous as all that sexual groping and pumping and flopping around might seem, it was the closest thing to divine union we had on this earth.

Paul had dreamed of kissing Ian's lips. He longed for it to be possible. Yet in his dreams, it had always been as singular and extraordinary for the young man as it was for Paul, an exception, not the rule. The angel had no experience, no past; in fact, Paul imagined the moment without any context at all. Now he realized it might be possible to have the real Ian in his life. But the price would be very high. He would have to give up the beautiful fantasy. The angel would have to come down to earth.

Ian could tell he'd made Paul uncomfortable, but he completely misjudged why.

"I guess you preach that it's a sin, 'men lying down with men,'" he said.

"Let he who is without sin…."

"So you do think it's a sin?"

"It's not something I preach about."

"You're a Christian, though, right? You think it's an 'abomination'?"

"You're quoting the Old Testament."

"The Bible. And in your church you believe that God wrote the Bible?"

"Men wrote the Bible. Inspired by God."

"So everything in it must be true, because God doesn't make mistakes?"

"I suppose. More or less."

"Well, if God doesn't want there to be gay people, and he went ahead and made them anyway, that seems like a pretty big mistake to me. One or the other has to be a mistake. They can't both be true."

"That's a good point. I think the church's position is that God made people with free will and they make their own choices."

"You think it's a choice?"

"I think that's the church's position."

"You're the minister. What do you say?"

"I don't know."

They continued riding for a moment in silence. Finally, Ian asked, "Are you married?"

"I was."

"So you've been in love, then, right? I mean, have you ever just looked at someone and felt like you were struck by lightning?"

Paul felt his heart race. Could Ian possibly know? "Yes," he said.

"Did you have a choice?"

Paul pulled into the church parking lot. He turned off the car and looked straight into Ian's eyes. "No," he said. "I didn't."

They held each other's gaze. Could the look have really been as long and significant as it felt to Paul?

Ian turned away and looked out the window at his own car. "I actually got it in a parking space. Pretty impressive."

"Do you usually drive when you've had that much to drink?" Paul asked.

Ian wrinkled his forehead, but he didn't answer the question directly. "I really need to stop," he said softly. "Sorry if I was…. Well, I mean, thanks again for everything." He started to pull the door handle.

"Wait!" Paul said, with a bit more urgency than he'd intended. He couldn't leave things the way they were, with Ian thinking Paul disapproved of him.

"I think, it seems like maybe we got off on a bad foot," he began. "I just hope you'll… please keep my number. Because I'd just rather you call me. I'd rather, if you were in a situation. Sometimes it helps to talk to somebody who's not part of your normal life. I mean, I'm not working on commission. I'm not trying to save a certain number of souls to win a trip to Tahiti." What on Earth was his mouth doing? "Maybe you're kind of embarrassed about how you were yesterday, but it's okay. You don't have anything to be ashamed of. I think you're very smart. A lot of people, they're too intimidated to talk to a minister like that."

"You're just a person, right?"

"Just like you. Keep my number. It's my cell. It's not the church. If anything goes wrong, you can reach me day or night. You can call me at two in the morning if you need to."

"Sure," Ian said as he got out of the car. "Thanks."

Paul could tell Ian never planned to come back, and he would not call.

As the days passed, Paul thought about Ian, but the thoughts took on a different character. It was not longing and desire but worry and concern that occupied him. He wondered why God would have made him aware of the young man and his troubles if He was not going to give him the power to do anything about it.

Ian was a beautiful, precious young man desperately in need of rescue. It pained Paul to have seen it. He was filled with a desire to act—to do something—but what could he do? If he saw someone being abused, he could not stand by and watch it happen. He would have to intervene. But in this case, the abuser and the abused lived in the same body.

Paul was a virtual stranger to Ian. There was no way the young man would accept his help if he offered it uninvited. He had to leave it in God's hands. That was the hardest thing to do. Why had God cursed him with knowing about Ian? Was this, after all, the moral of his angelic vision—futility? Impotence? Hadn't God done enough to impress that message upon him already?

In the end, all Paul could do was pray. "Take care of him, God. Help him find his way."

FAITH

There is a popular mythology about climbing mountains. An entire genre of inspirational books recounts a dangerous summit climb and the spiritual lessons gained from it. When they prepare for a summit push, mountaineers imagine the sense of elation and accomplishment at the peak. They imagine moments of reverence and spiritual revelation. But when they actually get there, most climbers are filled with nothing so much as a sense of exhaustion and the knowledge that a long and difficult journey still lies ahead. The mountain steadfastly refuses to conform to the stories we impose upon it.

PAUL WAS riding the back of an elephant as it went charging through the sanctuary of the church. He was afraid the animal might knock over the pews like so many dominoes. He pulled on the reins, trying to gain control, when he heard music playing. A generic cell phone ringtone.

"What?"

Paul sat straight up in bed. He looked at the clock. It was almost 2:00 a.m. Where was his cell phone? Paul rolled out of bed and went running toward the sound, nearly tripping over an end table along the way. He managed to reach the phone, in the kitchen, just before the voice mail picked up.

"Hello?" he said in a groggy voice.

"Hi, um, Paul? I don't know if you remember me. It's Ian. Ian Finnerty. You drove me home that one time."

"It's the middle of the night."

"Yeah, well, the thing is. I'm kind of… in jail. I didn't know who else to call."

This was not a call Paul ever, in his life, imagined he would be getting—the 2:00 a.m. "come bail me out of jail" call. God was really testing him with this angel. Paul got dressed, drove to the ATM half asleep, and took out $200 in cash. Then he drove to a part of town he rarely had cause to visit, especially not at 2:00 a.m. with a wallet full of cash.

Well, on the upside, now I know where the jail is, for future reference, he thought.

Ian sat in one corner of the cell with his feet on the long wooden bench and his knees curled up to his chest. His head was tilted down, hiding his face behind his long hair. It was the same position in which Paul had found him weeks ago sitting on the floor of the pavilion. The institutional green walls gave everything a pallid otherworldly appearance. Paul allowed himself a momentary daydream. If an angel ever did come to earth, maybe men would put it in a zoo for family entertainment and scientific study. It might look something like this.

"Hello, Ian," Paul said.

Ian glanced up. He blushed slightly. His eyebrows came up in the center, making his eyes appear larger, like a faun's.

"I kept your number," he said with an embarrassed smile. His expression was that of a wounded child and automatically generated sympathy. Paul wondered if the look was a well-rehearsed gambit by someone aware of his own beauty and accustomed to making use of it. If it was, it hardly lessened the effect.

Paul responded with his best imitation of a schoolteacher. "First time I've been called in the middle of the night to bail someone out of jail," he said.

"It's always an adventure with me. You said I could call at 2:00 a.m..... I guess you didn't think I would."

"Why didn't you call one of your friends?"

Ian rubbed the back of his neck. "I guess I've burned a few bridges."

Paul sighed. "I'd like to be your friend," he said, "but I have to know something."

"What?"

"You're sitting in a jail cell. Is this rock bottom for you, or do you have farther to go? Because if you do, I'm not sure I want to watch it."

Ian's eyes welled up. He pressed his lips together into a thin line. He didn't look away, nor did he answer.

"I can bail you out," Paul said. "I brought money. And I want to help you. But if you just want to get out of here so you can drink yourself to death, I'm not going to be part of that. You're better off here."

The tears escaped down Ian's cheeks, and he pulled his knees in tighter toward his chest. "I've tried," he said. "I want to stop. I really do."

"Do you mean that?"

"Yeah."

Paul nodded. "Then I'll help you."

Ian chewed on the nail of his left index finger. Paul noticed for the first time that his nails had already been gnawed almost to the nub. Paul described his plan.

"If you're serious, I'll bail you out. I'll even talk to the judge and see what we can work out," Paul said. "I'm willing to vouch for you if you're willing to commit to a rehab program."

"I want to. It's just…."

"What?"

"I mean, I've called those places," Ian said. "I can't afford it."

"Is that an excuse?"

"No. It's the truth. They're not cheap."

"Then I'll help you."

"I don't know."

"If you want your life to change, I'm offering you a way out," Paul said. "If you don't want it to change, that's fine. Stay here. It's up to you. This is the important part. If you agree to this, we have to do it now. Tonight. We'll go back to your apartment, pack up what you need. You can stay at my house tonight. Tomorrow I'll make some calls and find a place that can take you right away, before you change your mind. Are you willing to do that?"

Ian was in no position to argue.

"Yeah," he said.

Paul paid Ian's bail and drove him back to the brick-block dwelling. As it happened, it was rather conveniently located to the jail, only a couple of blocks away, in the same ugly section of town. (Ian's car was not an immediate problem. The police had impounded it and would not release it until after the case came to court.) Paul parked and got out. He made a point to lock the car, something he didn't bother doing in his own driveway.

Ian fiddled with his keys. "It's a little tricky," he said. He turned the handle of the heavy gray door to the left and to the right. He jiggled the key, turned it again, and finally it swung open. "Oh, if you ever come here, the buzzer doesn't work," he said. "My window's in the front. You have to knock on it. Most people just call with a cell phone."

Inside was a dark, narrow corridor. Ian produced a second key and opened the door to his unit. "Home sweet home," he said.

The apartment was just about the smallest Paul had ever seen. It was laid out like two walk-in closets in an inverted L shape. The living room portion had a fold-out sofa—which was apparently Ian's bed—a small folding table, and an old television resting on the floor. There was only one decoration. Taped to the back of the door was a picture of a mountain, which had been ripped out of a 1998 calendar. The second part of the L was the kitchen, which doubled as the entryway. Tacked onto the end of the kitchen was a bathroom small enough that the only way to walk through it was sideways. Sitting on the edge of a counter, which was barely wider than the sink and stove, was a bottle of Jack Daniels with about a fourth remaining.

"Did you drink all of that yourself?" Paul asked.

"Who else?" Ian shrugged.

"You drank it all tonight?"

"You ask a lot of questions," Ian said. He opened the bottle and poured the remaining contents into the sink and dumped the bottle into the brown paper bag that contained the trash. He turned and saw Paul's expression of triumph at the gesture.

Ian gave a half smile. "Don't get too excited," he said. "I've done this before."

"Well, hopefully you won't have to do it again," Paul said.

Ian grabbed a green backpack from the sofa, reached underneath, and pulled out a cardboard box that contained his clothing. As he was throwing underwear and shirts into the bag, Paul looked in Ian's cabinets. There were three packets of ramen noodles, a box of macaroni and cheese, and a can of tomato soup. In the refrigerator were half a bottle of orange juice and a bottle of ketchup.

Ian seemed to know what Paul was looking for. "You're looking for more booze?" he asked.

"Sorry," Paul said, "I just wanted...."

"It's okay," Ian said. "I wouldn't trust me either. It's hidden in the water tank in the back of the toilet."

Paul went into the miniature bathroom, lifted the top off the tank, and discovered a bottle of rum hidden there. Paul brought it back to the kitchen so Ian could dump it out too.

"Is that all of it now?" Paul asked.

"Yeah," Ian said as he opened the bottle and dumped its contents in the sink.

On the ride to Paul's apartment, Ian sat in the passenger seat with the green backpack on his lap. He clutched it to him like a child might hold a stuffed toy. It fascinated Paul that Ian, who lived in such a terrible environment, would be so trusting. He had just put his fate entirely into the hands of a near stranger. Then again, he hadn't been given a lot of choice. The alternative was to stay in jail. As if sensing Paul's thoughts, Ian broke the silence.

"Why are you helping me like this?" he asked.

"I suppose it's part of my faith."

"Oh."

"What?"

"No, that's cool."

"I remember. You said you and the church were divorced."

"I said that?"

"Yeah. The first time I drove you home. I know you don't remember it."

"I don't know. I've just met a lot of Christians who were pretty ugly. My mom was a 'good Christian.' She threw me out of the house."

"Why?"

"She didn't like my boyfriend."

"Why?"

"He was a guy."

"Oh."

"She's going to Heaven and I'm going to Hell with my 'worthless drunk' old man."

"How old were you?"

"Seventeen."

"Not all Christians think that way, you know. Jesus preached about forgiveness, not damning people."

"What about those guys with the signs 'God Hates Fags'?"

"God doesn't hate. You shouldn't lump us all in together. Just because they call themselves Christians.... I don't want to be associated with that. Most Christians don't."

"I think I believe in God. But that word 'faith'...."

"What about it?"

"It's like 'listen to whatever I say and don't question it.' I don't like that."

"You don't understand faith the way I do."

"So what is it?"

"Faith isn't about believing things that aren't true because some authority told you to do it. It's about trusting in things that are true, even if you aren't in a position to prove it. Sometimes you have to believe in something before you can see it…. I have faith in you."

The corners of Ian's lips curled up into the distinctive smile that Paul loved so much. "Are you going to do a sermon about me this Sunday? The sinner you bailed out of jail?"

"You're not a sinner," Paul said firmly. "You have an addiction. God doesn't damn people for being sick."

Ian chewed on his lip for a moment. "It would be cool, though," he said, "if you wrote a sermon about me. That stuff about faith. I'd come and listen."

"If that will get you into church, I'll do it."

"I want to help you win that trip to Tahiti."

"If I do, I'll take you with me."

"Deal."

After Sara died, Paul couldn't stand to be in the house they had bought together. It had too many memories, too many ghosts. There were the happy memories, of course, like the day he had carried her in across the vestibule to mark their new life together, the wallpaper in the bathroom that Sara had picked out herself and curiously hated—a source of constant playful teasing—and the plans they had made together at night in bed. All those joyful moments had been rendered painful by the loss of Sara.

Like the guest room that they had planned to one day make into a nursery, each room contained dreams of a future that would now never be. The kitchen table would now always be the place he'd been sitting when she gave him the news about her diagnosis. The bathroom off the master bedroom was now the place where Paul had cleaned up the vomit and scooped the strands of red hair from the sinks and the drains. The sofa in the front room was where he sat in a daze and met with the many church members who came to bring him hot meals and sympathy. He couldn't face any of it.

He bought a modest two-bedroom condominium. The master bedroom contained a dresser and a king-sized bed. The second bedroom Paul filled with books and made into his study. The living room was open and airy and underfurnished. There was a black futon, a matching chair, and a wide-screen TV in a wall-mounted shelving unit.

Even though Paul had lived in the condo for some time, Ian would be his first overnight guest. Paul was about to apologize for how small his home was when he remembered Ian's apartment.

"Wow," Ian said, looking around. "This is a great place."

"Thanks," Paul said. "I don't have a guest room, but the futon folds out. I hope that will be okay. It's comfortable."

"This is great," he said. "Is this your wife?"

Although Paul had moved to escape Sara's ghost, he had decorated his new place almost entirely with framed photos of her— their wedding, their honeymoon travels, early dates they'd gone on together.

"Sara," he said.

"She's pretty."

"Thanks," Paul said. It seemed like the appropriate answer, although it was odd to thank someone for a compliment about someone else—as though Sara's looks were his achievement.

"So you're not together now?"

Paul hated those kinds of questions. He hated to have to give the answer, to make the other person uncomfortable. He hated that moment after they said, "I'm sorry," when they would both stand for a few seconds in quiet reverence. He never felt like his response was quite right.

"Cancer," he said.

"That sucks," Ian said.

The unexpected blunt answer made Paul smile. "You're right. It does."

As Paul unfolded the futon, Ian kicked off his shoes and pulled off his socks. Next he reached over his head and pulled off his T-shirt. Paul willed himself not to watch. He busied himself with the sheets. Tucking them in, straightening them. Straightening them some more. He heard the metal clank of Ian unbuckling his belt. Paul arranged the pillows.

"You don't have to do that," Ian said. Shirt off. Belt unbuckled. Jeans slightly unzipped. "I can make the bed."

Paul straightened the sheets some more. Hospital corners, maybe he should try to do hospital corners. *What are hospital corners, anyway?* "Do you think you'll have enough blankets?"

"Oh yeah. Definitely. You really don't need to make a fuss." He slid his jeans down over his narrow hips and stepped out of them. He was now wearing nothing but a pair of blue briefs, and Paul made a new discovery. Ian had a tattoo. It seemed to be some kind of leaf or a vertical Celtic knot. Just the top of the design was peeking out from the briefs on Ian's right hip bone. It drew Paul's eye downward. Gave him permission to stare at....

In an instant, a whole scene played out in his mind. He would ask about the tattoo, come in close, and inch the briefs down, slowly, to see the rest of the image. And what would happen next? Paul knew that tattoo and its placement were going to invade his thoughts day and night. He couldn't help it. It was completely inevitable. And he hated it. He knew this was exactly what it had been designed to do. How many men had seen the full design? How many had acted out the very scene Paul had just scripted in his mind?

"Well, I hope you have a good sleep. You have a big day tomorrow."

"Yeah," Ian said a bit nervously as he climbed under the covers. "Good night, Paul. Thanks for rescuing me."

The next morning, Paul got up early. He sat at the computer researching alcoholism treatment centers and making phone calls trying to find one that could take Ian right away. From his study, he could see the futon and watch Ian sleep. As soon as he seemed to stir, Paul got up, went to the kitchen, and came back with a glass of water. He sat down at the foot of the futon.

Ian sat up, squinted, and looked around to get his bearings. When he saw Paul, he smiled with recognition. His hair was tangled, and there were slight dark circles under his eyes.

"I figured you'd be thirsty," Paul said, handing him the glass of water.

"Thanks," Ian said. He took the glass, gulped down the water, and handed it, empty, back to Paul.

"Do you need more? I have aspirin too if you need any."

"No, I'm okay," he said as he tried to undo a knot in his hair with his fingers. "You seem like you've done this before."

"What, brought a man home from jail?"

"No," Ian said, blushing slightly. "I mean, maybe you know something about… drunks."

"I'm playing this by ear," he said. "You remember what we talked about last night?"

"Yeah, this time I remember."

"You still want to do this?"

"Yeah." He sounded nervous but committed.

"Well, get dressed. I'll make some breakfast and we can go."

HUNTINGTON HOSPITAL

Mount Rainier rises ten thousand feet from its base to the heavens. Its massive cap of snow and ice flows contains as much frozen water as the twelve other Cascade volcanoes combined. Each year, ten thousand people try to test their limits by scaling the massive peak. About half will not succeed.

The climbers with their ropes and crampons and supplemental oxygen tanks fascinated Paul. How does one prepare for an adventure so complete that he might never return? If a climber returns, he comes back internally changed, with his limitations and boundaries forever shifted, and yet outwardly he is entirely the same.

FROM THE outside, the Huntington Hospital for Alcoholism and Addiction Treatment looked like a small college or a country day school. Set on a vast landscape of rolling hills, the defining features of its campus were a large white building that looked like a farmhouse and a cozy white chapel with a large steeple. Once inside, however, it looked more like what it was—a hospital. There was a reception area with a gray institutional tile floor, a small seating area with the familiar collection of waiting room magazines, and a sliding-glass window dividing the staff from the visitors. During Sara's cancer treatment, Paul had developed a strange relationship with hospitals—a mix of distaste and relaxed familiarity.

"I'm here to see Ian Finnerty," he told the receptionist.

"Just a moment," she said. She flipped through a tabbed binder under *F*, put her finger on his name, and then walked to the back of the room. Next, Paul heard her voice over the hospital speakers.

"Ian F., Ian F., please come to reception. You have a visitor. Ian F., Ian F."

Paul sat down in one of the chairs to wait. He was holding a gift for Ian. Flowers had seemed inappropriate, but he wanted to bring something. He had settled on a small potted plant, a Venus flytrap. He sat up straight as he waited, and his legs shook. He was aware of his physical presence in the chair and wanted to seat himself so he would project the right image when Ian first saw him. He was shuffling in his seat, trying to find the best comfortable pose, when the door swung open. There it was, the face that had existed every day in his imagination, now in front of him in real physical form. Ian's eyes were bright and alert, and he was taller than Paul had remembered. He wasn't hanging his head anymore.

"Hi," Ian said. He smiled broadly, revealing the little gap in his front teeth.

Paul's pupils dilated. "You look great," he said. "Here." He thrust the plant at Ian.

"What is it?"

"I brought you something. It's…."

Ian raised one eyebrow. "You brought me a fly-eating plant?"

"I was looking at the plants in the shop, and I thought you might like one that actually does something. I thought it might be more interesting for you."

Ian held it up at eye level and looked at it from all angles. "Does it have a name?"

"It's a plant."

"I think I'll call it 'Fido.' Come on, Fido! Let's go to my room. I'll show you your new home."

They went through the swinging doors and down another antiseptic hallway. Ian greeted everyone he passed by name. "Hi, Heather. Hi, Joe. This is my friend, Paul." *My friend.*

"Wow, you know everyone," Paul said.

"There's something about being the same kind of freak that tends to bring people together."

"Hmm. Maybe, but I think it's you."

"Oh, I have a joke," Ian said. "Want to hear my joke?"

"Sure."

"An Irishman walks into a bar…. Do you like it so far?"

"I think I've heard this story."

"So this Irishman goes into the bar, and every night he orders three glasses of whiskey. The bartender asks, 'Why do you always get three glasses?' The guy says, 'I get one for me and two for my brothers in America.' So one night he comes in and he only orders two drinks. The bartender says, 'I'm sorry about the loss of your brother.' And the Irishman says, 'Oh no, my brothers are fine. It's just that I quit drinking.'"

They arrived at the elevator, and Ian pushed the button. "It's an alcoholism joke," he said. "I heard that one in group." They looked up at the lights over the elevator door. "I like group. People tell their horror stories, and you listen to them one after the other and you say, 'Well, at least I never did that.' Makes you feel better about yourself."

The up arrow illuminated with a ding, and the elevator doors slid open. Once they had stepped inside, Ian said, "There was this one guy in group, he was staying in all these shit-bag hotels. He said, 'Happiness was checking into a hotel and not finding pubic hair on the bar of soap.'"

"That's disgusting," Paul said.

"Yeah, but it's kind of poetic too, don't you think? You've never checked into a motel and found, like, a used syringe in the middle of the floor?"

"Uh, no."

"That doesn't happen so much at the Hilton, huh?"

"Hardly ever."

The elevator arrived at the third floor. "Come on," Ian said, "let's go show Fido his new home."

Ian's room was also hospital-cold and antiseptic. It had its own bathroom, complete with wheelchair railings. There were two hospital beds with a pair of small rolling tables designed for bedridden and postoperative patients to eat their Jell-O. Ian's bed was on the far side of the room near the window. He set the fly-eating plant down on his rolling table. "Here you are, Fido. Look for flies! Go on! I don't think he sees any. Do you think I have to feed it if it doesn't catch anything?"

"I don't think so," Paul said. "But you can feed it hamburger if you want. It will eat that."

"I don't have a great history of taking care of things."

Ian talked about the channels on the television, his roommate, Gary—an aging rock musician—and the controls that made the bed sit up and recline. Paul's mind was still back in the elevator with hypodermic needles and pubic hairs on soap. He was trying to reconcile who he believed Ian to be with the life he must have led. Ian had such a warm and open energy. He was playful and exuded a childlike innocence. How could someone like that have seen the kind of ugliness he described? How had anyone let that happen?

"You wanna see the grounds?" Ian asked. "It's the best part. Anyway, I need a cigarette. They don't let you smoke in the building."

"Imagine that."

"I know. They're a bunch of fascists, right?"

"Maybe you should quit."

"Well, one addiction at a time. I have to kick my heroin habit first."

Paul's jaw dropped.

"That was a joke," Ian said.

"Right. Sorry."

Once they were outside the building, the clinical nature of the property disappeared. The grounds were quiet and serene, with a long winding path through flowers and trees. It circled around a gazebo and ended at a duck pond full of lilies, surrounded by weeping willows. It seemed like an exclusive country club or a vacation retreat. Ian took out a cigarette, lit it, and took a long drag. "Fresh air," he said.

"It's beautiful here," Paul said.

"Enjoy the shakes and hallucinations in a lovely natural setting," Ian said. "I think that's what it says in the guidebook."

"Did you have that? Shakes and hallucinations?"

"The first week I was cursing you the whole time," Ian said. "Fucking, fucking bastard do-gooder, son-of-a-bitch minister. Why couldn't he mind his own fucking business?"

Paul smiled. People hardly ever swore in front of a minister without apologizing. He found it refreshing.

"You see the duck pond?" Ian asked. "When I was still in the medical wing, the ducks somehow got in, and I came out of my room and there was this parade of ducks walking straight down the hall. There was this other guy standing there, and I looked at him, and he looked at me. He said, 'Do you see ducks?' I thought, 'Thank God!'"

"So it was bad?" Paul asked.

"I've had better times."

"Are you still cursing me?"

"Well, you brought me a plant that eats flies, which is kind of weird, so I guess you're okay." He took another long drag on the cigarette and blew the smoke out through one side of his mouth.

"You could have checked yourself out if you wanted to."

"Now he tells me! No, really, I didn't want to."

"You look much better. You really look great." *Am I gushing too much about his looks?* Paul wondered.

They sat down at a picnic table with a view of the pond. The sun's rays illuminated the right side of Ian's face, making his features more soft and delicate. His eyes, in this light, seemed more green than blue. The light and shadow, the green of his eyes contrasted with the green of the willows—Paul wondered what classical artist could best have captured this scene.

"You know what I learned?" Ian asked, sucking on his cigarette and blowing the smoke out of his nose. *So much for the classical masters.* "They said that when one spouse is an alcoholic, the husbands usually end up leaving, but the wives usually stick it out. What do you think that says?"

"I don't know."

"Men are selfish shits, that's what I think," he said, gazing off into the woods. "They say, 'This isn't fun for me anymore,' and they take off."

Paul laughed. "We're not still talking about husbands and wives, are we?"

Ian tucked a strand of hair behind his ear and let his fingers run all the way down through the long tresses. "It's okay," he said. "I probably would have dumped me too if I'd been dating myself."

Paul wished he could tell Ian what he was thinking: *I wouldn't.*

Ian rested his chin on his palm with the cigarette between his index and second fingers, his pinky dangling in the corner of his mouth so he could chew absentmindedly on the much-abused nail. *Two bad habits for the price of one*, Paul thought. He laughed to himself.

"What?" Ian asked.

"Nothing," he said.

They gazed at each other for a moment with curiosity. It seemed as if they had just shared a secret, but Paul could not be sure what the secret was.

"I think you're different," Ian said. "I bet if your wife was alcoholic, you'd stick around."

"Why do you think so?"

"Well, you're here. You seem like that kind of guy. A good guy."

Paul shrugged. "I'm a minister. It's my job to be a good guy."

"Come on! Not all ministers are good guys."

"No, but it makes it easier. Being a minister gives you permission to help people. Do you know what I mean? People are so suspicious of each other most of the time. They're afraid to accept help because they suspect the other person has ulterior motives. But if you're a minister, and you want to help someone, they might let you. That's one of the best things about the job. Having permission to be a good guy without people suspecting you."

"Like with me, right?" He puffed again on the cigarette and squinted as the smoke wafted into his eyes. "I should…. I've been joking around, but… thank you."

"You don't have to thank me. I'm just happy to see you doing well. That's a present for me."

"You see that building over there?" Ian pointed with the two fingers that held his cigarette. "That's where they keep the priests. They have a special wing for clergy."

"I didn't realize there were that many alcoholic priests."

"Loads. They can't have sex, you know, so they just sit around drinking communion wine and they end up here."

"We do grape juice at my church."

"Do you believe it actually turns into the blood of Christ?"

"No, it's symbolic."

"I think the Catholics believe it actually turns into blood. It's like cannibalism. Isn't that kind of creepy, drinking blood?"

"We're only symbolic cannibals."

"I don't get it, though. I'm not trying to be, you know, critical. I just don't understand. I mean… isn't cannibalism a bad thing?"

"I can't speak for the Catholics, but in my church, we don't believe in the transubstantiation."

"The what?"

"When the bread and wine are literally transformed into flesh and blood. In our church, it's for remembrance. It reenacts the Last Supper. So it honors Christ's sacrifice. And it's one of the few traditions we have that Jesus actually set into motion himself. He didn't put up a Christmas tree. So it goes all the way back. That is amazing to me, every time, to think about people performing this same ritual for centuries. You're part of this long stream of time, of generations."

"Okay, I can see re-creating the Last Supper, but why drink Jesus's blood?"

"That's always seemed very powerful to me, the blood. Just the whole physical nature of it. Did you know that some Romans thought the blood contained the soul? They saw that when people died they lost their color, so they figured their animating spirit must be in the blood. So if you drink from that cup, it's making Jesus a part of you, not just in your mind, in your spirit, but in your body. So he's part of your physical being and your everyday life."

"In your body…. I just…. It sounds nice but I don't really know what that means."

"That's okay."

"No, but I'm not putting it down. I'm interested. It means something to you. I'm trying to understand why."

"I don't want to preach to you. I don't want you to think that's why I'm here."

"You're not. I'm asking."

"Okay, the body of Christ. Well, it's about being nourished by his sacrifice. You're making the essence of Christ part of you. It's about destruction and rebirth. The way the tree that falls in the woods decays and nourishes the flowers. Jesus was a man and existed in a physical body, but he doesn't anymore. But now he exists in all our bodies. He keeps living in us. Christianity is about resurrection. Or at least it is for me. Different churches focus on different parts of the story. The cross, it's a difficult symbol because it was what the Romans used for torture, but it's been transformed. Now it's a symbol of resurrection. What I think that means—one thing I think that means—is that everyone has a chance to be reborn. You don't have to get it right the first time. You start where you are. Everybody deserves a second chance."

"Hmm," Ian said. He turned his eyes upward to the left and took another drag on his cigarette. He was thinking about what Paul had said, and he seemed to like what he heard.

"You told me your mother was religious. What kind of church did you go to?"

"Pentecostal. Real fire-and-brimstone stuff."

"Wow."

"It was all about Christ's army and going to war with the devil. You wanted to be on the right side of the war."

"Did people speak in tongues?"

"Yeah. They'd lift up their arms to God and cry and fall on the floor and babble."

"Did you?"

"Yeah, I did it too," he said, glancing at the ash of his cigarette.

Paul tried to imagine a young Ian on his knees, his arms uplifted to heaven, with tears streaming down his face, babbling incoherently for the Lord. Paul had always had a certain fascination with Pentecostalism. There was something uncomfortable and disturbing about it, and yet he admired and longed for the Pentecostals' completely immersive, emotional relationship to the divine.

His own religious tradition was so comfortable and staid. Respectable people stood at neat pews; they read prayers in an inflectionless monotone. They opened their hymnals and sang "Hallelujah" in an oddly flat and soulless way (though every church had one or two choir members who loved to belt out the high notes and harmonies.) His church's European heritage expressed reverence in hushed tones and quiet contemplation. It did not make noise. It was an antidote for the flashing lights and frenzy of rush-hour traffic and evening TV. Yet he also wished he could feel worship in his guts. He admired the call-and-response of the black Baptist churches and the energy of a gospel choir, and he wanted to be so swept away that he couldn't express it in true language, like the Pentecostals did.

"What did it feel like?" Paul asked. "Did you feel like you were having a spiritual experience?"

"Mmm. I guess, sometimes. You get wrapped up in it. Everyone is around, and there's all the music and energy and people dancing. You feel the energy. At the time I thought that was, like, God energy. Now I think it was just adrenaline, you know? I just didn't want people to think I was with the devil. I was putting on a show. I knew I was damned to Hell."

"Why?"

"Leviticus 18:22. The inerrant word of God." Ian gave a rueful look, crushed out his cigarette, and took another out of the pack.

"Is that the one about…?"

"'A man shall not lie down with a man as with a woman. It is an abomination.'"

"I can't believe you memorized chapter and verse on that."

"My personal verse."

"Did you really believe that? That you were going to Hell?"

"My mom believed it. She believed in evil forces. Like the devil was hiding in the bushes just waiting to grab you. If you didn't fight him off, you know, he'd drag you down. Like with the couch. We had this couch. See, we lost everything in a fire when I was thirteen. So we moved into this little apartment, but we didn't have any furniture or anything. So this really nice woman across the street gave us a couch. It was this old beige thing, smelled like incense. Me and a friend lugged it up the stairs. Well, then the woman invited us over for dinner one time, and my mom saw that she had a Ouija board on the shelf. She absolutely flipped out. The devil was in that house. We had to leave right away. We couldn't even finish dinner, and I wasn't supposed to talk to the woman anymore. And we had to get rid of the couch too, of course, because the devil was in it. It was contaminated. This guy from the church brought over a pickup truck, and I helped him lug it back down the stairs and load it, and he took it to the dump. So we had to go back to watching TV sitting on folding chairs. It was just stupid. When she found out I was gay, she probably thought the couch did it."

"What happened?"

"When?"

"When she found out?"

"Oh. It… it wasn't pretty."

"I'm sorry." There was a brief lull. "Have you tried to talk to her since?"

"Yeah, right." Ian quickly changed the subject. "So now I'm going to do community service in a church. Ironic, right?"

"Well, it's not so ironic. Things happen for a reason. I'm thinking… no, forget it."

"What?"

"Well, maybe God wants you back."

"Maybe."

Paul drove home filled with a warm glow. He had learned more than he had ever expected about Ian in one afternoon. He finally felt he could say that he knew the young man, that they were friends. Ian's life was much different than Paul had imagined, but he never went back and revised his image completely, starting from scratch. Instead, he built upon the impression he already had. He was fleshing out the biography of "Ian the Angel." Every new fact was interpreted in that light. This allowed him to see a side of Ian that others often missed, for all this was true about him: he was a chain-smoking alcoholic who used coarse language and had sex with men without ever catching their names. He was also a beautiful soul, warm and positive, compassionate and bright, an innocent who longed to be loved.

IT WAS not unusual for people to come to the church to perform community service. What was unusual was for the minister to take a personal interest in them. Usually they called and Julie found some tasks for them to do, signed their papers, and sent them on their way.

Ian was different. Two weeks before he was to be released from treatment, Paul started talking to Julie about what sort of jobs they might have for him. Hardly a day went by without Paul making some statement about Ian's upcoming service work:

"There are a lot of leaves on the playground. You could have Ian rake them," Paul said. "You know," he said, "I noticed that the fence by the third-grade classroom needs repair. Maybe that's something Ian could do." "Maybe we could have Ian check the books in the children's library and make sure they're in alphabetical order."

In the lunchroom, Paul told the staff about visiting Ian in the hospital and how well he was doing. He spoke in great detail about helping Ian sell his car. (Ian didn't think he needed it anymore after losing his license for his driving offense.) And he mentioned several times that he would be driving Ian to the church himself. When Ian actually arrived with Paul on a Wednesday afternoon, he was nearly a celebrity.

When she saw Ian, Julie sat up straighter and her eyes grew wide. She brushed a nonexistent strand of hair from her forehead. "I'm Julie," she said.

Emily and Marlee were soon standing at the desk as well. Marlee giggled when she introduced herself. Emily played with her hair.

"Hi, I'm Ian," he said, nodding his head slightly. He seemed uncharacteristically shy. In his zeal to introduce Ian to the staff, Paul had forgotten the whole thing might be uncomfortable for him. He was, after all, there to do community service for drunk driving. It wasn't the kind of situation where a person normally tried to draw attention to himself. Paul suddenly wished he had talked a bit less. He put a hand on Ian's shoulder and directed him away from the women.

"Here," he said, "I'll show you what we have for you to do."

Paul sent Ian out to rake the grounds and came back inside. The women in the office were still huddled.

"Don't forget, you're married!" Emily was saying when Paul came into earshot.

"But I'm not dead!" Julie said. "And don't forget, you have Bob."

"Who's Bob?" Emily said, giggling. "Marlee's single."

"He's too good-looking for me," Marlee said. "Those cute ones are always trouble. They always know how good-looking they are. They're heartbreakers."

"He could break my heart," Emily said.

"I'm telling you," Marlee said, "the good-looking ones are always trouble, especially the cute ones. They're the worst."

"Ooh, look," Julie said. "He's raking by the window."

"I guess it doesn't hurt to look, though," Marlee added with a grin.

Paul put his hands on his hips and struck a mock-managerial pose. "Don't you people have work to do?" He was enjoying their conversation as much as they were. Their appreciation of Ian's beauty reinforced his own impressions. What made it even more fun for Paul was that he was the only one in the room who knew how futile their gazing was. He was surprised at how much pleasure he took in sharing a secret with Ian.

"Oh, Paul," Julie said. "You just don't understand."

Paul hummed a little tune as he went into his office.

The Phone Call

"Suppose a Man was carried asleep out of a plain Country amongst the Alps and left there upon the Top of one of the highest Mountains, when he wak'd and look'd about him, he wou'd think himself in an inchanted Country, or carried into another world; every Thing wou'd appear to him so different to what he had ever seen or imagin'd before."
　　　　　—Thomas Burnet, The Sacred Theory of the Earth, *1684*

THE NEXT evening, Paul was sitting in front of the television. He wasn't so much "watching" as passing the time. When his cell phone rang, he picked up the remote and hit the mute button. He flipped open the phone without looking at the name of the caller.

"Hi, it's Ian Finnerty." Ian's voice was familiar, yet also deeper than Paul remembered it, much more masculine than it seemed when looking at his face.

"How are you doing?" Paul asked, sitting up straight. "Are you in trouble?"

"No. I'm fine. Well, I really want a drink."

"You're not going to, are you?"

"I thought maybe I'd call you instead."

"I'm glad you did," Paul said as he picked up the remote and turned off the TV. "Is anything wrong?"

"No, nothing's wrong. You know, except for the alcoholism thing. It's just that all my habits involve drinking. Turn on the TV, pour a drink. That kind of thing. It's been a long time."

"How long?"

"Like… ten years, I guess."

"Ten years? Didn't you say you were twenty-four?"

"Yeah."

"You started drinking at fourteen?"

"Yeah, but not seriously. I really got into the swing of things at… probably seventeen. Like, beginning at sixteen and heavily at seventeen."

"Wow."

"I was, what do you call it? A prodigy."

"I guess. How did you manage to start so young?"

"The devil made me do it."

"No, seriously."

"Boredom, I guess. No one was watching me."

"Where was your mother?" Paul asked, hoping he didn't sound judgmental.

"She worked two jobs. The rest of the time she was too busy hating my 'worthless drunk' dad and being in Christ's army to pay much attention to anything else."

"That must have been hard."

"I don't know. I guess. It's the only life I had. I don't have anything else to compare it to. Anyway, now I don't know how to do anything sober."

Paul lay down on the futon with his feet up on a pillow, preparing for a long conversation. "Do you miss going out to the places you used to drink? Seeing the people you used to drink with?"

"No, not really. I never really liked that much. I just went to the clubs when I was short on cash. Of course, that was most of the time, so I went a lot."

"Short on cash? Aren't they more expensive?"

"Yeah, if you're buying. But, you know, I have a pretty good face. I could always find someone to buy me a drink." *So he did know he was beautiful.*

"Did they expect you to go home with them?"

"Sometimes, but you don't really have to go home. They have these back rooms."

"Don't tell me about that!"

"I forgot. You're a minister. You have virgin ears. They didn't teach you about gay backroom sex in the seminary?"

"I just can't picture you like that."

"Yeah, I know. I look innocent."

"But is that what you wanted? Anonymous sex? You didn't want more than that?"

"Sure. I wanted alcohol."

There didn't seem to be much more to say on that topic. In the brief lull, Paul let his mind wander to how he must seem to Ian. "It's funny how people think ministers have 'virgin ears,'" he said. "We hear everything. A lot of people have secret lives."

"Like what?" Ian seemed delighted. "Give me some dirt."

"No, I can't do that," Paul said with a smile. "It's just that people's lives are so much more complicated than they seem to be on the surface. People are always putting on a show for each other."

"I know what you mean."

"Have you ever read the Bible?"

"You trying to save my soul again?"

"No, I just mean have you actually read it?"

"Bits and pieces."

"I hate it when people talk about it like it's a neat little rule book for living, all clean and shiny. It's full of every side of life. Good things happen to bad people, bad things happen to good people. People are awful to each other in the Bible. They're murderous and vengeful and ugly. But sometimes they're beautiful and compassionate. It is so rich. It's the whole messy human experience. If it was just red-haired, blue-eyed Jesus and pastel shepherds and the Ten Commandments, it wouldn't be so relevant. A lot of people think they're living their lives according to the Bible, and they've never read it. Every time I read it, I'm seeing it with different eyes. I read it from a different place, and it speaks to me in a different way."

"We just went from gay sex to the Bible in thirty seconds. That has to be some kind of record."

"You think we could get in Guinness?"

"You think they have that category?"

Paul laughed. "I'm really glad you called," he said. "I like talking to you. I was going to mention, if you're looking for a job—you're doing a good job on the community service. I'm sure it's not your 'calling'—you probably have lots of talents—but we're looking for a custodian full time if you're interested."

"A lot of talents? I only have one talent. Opening whiskey bottles. I'm not very good at closing them, though. I don't have a lot of practice at that. Or is that something you're not supposed to mention in a job interview?"

"Well, the job is yours if you want it."

"I'm going to go back to my high school guidance counselor and tell her that everything she said about interviewing was wrong. Just talk about backroom sex and your drinking problem and you got the gig."

"Yeah, at the church! I'll tell Julie to put you on the payroll as soon as your community service is finished."

"Thanks, boss."

"You want to know a secret? Callings are overrated. If you think you know what you're supposed to be doing, you just feel like you're not doing it well enough. Like God has a grand plan for you and you're failing to live up to it. If you don't know what you want to do, you still think God has a great plan for you and you're just not seeing it. Basically, I think we're all doomed."

"Doomed? You mean to fail God?"

"Failing God? Hmm. I'm not sure if that's what I mean. I'll have to think about that one."

IAN AND Paul talked for two more hours. Most of it was about nothing at all: television programs, movies, and the health of Fido the fly-eating plant. They would have talked longer, but they were both starting to fall asleep.

The next morning Paul drove over to Ian's apartment to take him to the church for his community service. Ian's familiar face took on new dimensions and personality as Paul reconnected it to the disembodied voice he'd spoken to on the phone.

The sermon topic that Sunday was "Failing God: Living Up to Your True Calling."

OVER THE next few weeks, Ian and Paul spoke on the phone two or three times a week, never for less than an hour. It was almost always Ian who called. At first he introduced himself by saying, "Hi, it's Ian," and using the excuse that he was afraid he was going to drink. But soon the conversations began, "Hi, it's me." No reason for the call was necessary. Paul looked forward to the calls and planned for them, keeping a mental catalog of interesting anecdotes from his day. He started to view everything in his life through the lens of how he would recount it to Ian when he called. He found himself taking a greater interest in his environment and the events of his own life and examining them from an entirely new perspective.

Ian had no pretense. He rarely censored himself, and he could say the most outrageous things at times with complete innocence because his intention was never to be shocking or provocative. The material, physical, and sensual world delighted him. He liked to talk about foods and their flavors, recounted memories complete with smells and textures, and he was completely matter-of-fact about sexuality. (And wouldn't an angel who descended to earth and took human form be delighted in the physical world around him?) He brought Paul out of the clouds, back to the Earth.

The church community came to know Ian as "that kid Paul is helping out." Gossip traveled fast through the church's unofficial newswire. Everyone knew how Ian had come to work at the church, that Paul had found him drunk in the pavilion and taken a personal interest in his recovery. It was obvious that Paul and the new custodian had a special relationship. Paul simply did not have enough craft to hide his affection. His face lit up whenever Ian walked in the room. His conversation was peppered with references to Ian, and Ian's with references to Paul. The two had inside jokes and could communicate with facial expressions and gestures instead of words. But the few church members who made the connection between the young man and Paul's newfound inspiration connected the events in reverse. They assumed helping Ian was a symptom and not the cause of Paul's new enthusiasm. Everyone believed Paul thought of Ian as the son he and Sara never had.

PAUL'S CHILDHOOD

If Mount Rainier is sublime in its nearly infinite scale, what do you call a place like Kansas? Farmland might have failed to capture the imagination of mystics and poets, but a landscape that flat creates its own infinity—an endless horizon. Kansas seems to have no end. When you're in the middle of it, you can see nothing else at all.

PAUL TOBIT'S hometown, Faller's Field, Kansas, was barely a dot on the map. In fact, had it been close to any other city, it would probably not have shown up on the map at all. Driving to Faller's was a straight shot, three hours through the corn on two-lane highways from the next largest city. You came into town past a billboard for Bob's Guns and Ammo, followed by another billboard advertising vacation Bible school. Then you turned when you got to a barn painted with a huge smiley face. "Hi Joe and Gertie," it said. (Paul always wondered if the message was to Joe and Gertie, or from Joe and Gertie.) Finally, down the hill to Faller's single stoplight. The metropolis of downtown Faller's Field consisted of one long road of little shops. There was the drug store, a sporting-goods store, a bar, a town museum—which it was unlikely anyone ever visited—a post office, and, of course, the stoplight.

Above it all, however, there was the one sign that they were part of the real world—the building. It had all the presence of the Sears Tower. It was a monolith, a huge brown square with "The Travelers" written across the top. It was called The Travelers because it moved. If Paul was on the school playground, it was there. When he looked out of his bedroom window, it was there. He truly believed that building was magic, and if it chose to follow Paul, there must have been something pretty special about him.

Of course, as an adult, he understood that his magic building had "Travelers" written across the top because it housed the offices of Traveler's Insurance. He also came to realize it wasn't that big a building; eight stories, if that. And it never really followed Paul; it only seemed to because it was the tallest building around. It was nothing personal. Anyone could see it from anyplace in town. Just like the mountain. It followed everyone, regardless of who that person was or what he did.

Paul was the son of Joe Tobit, owner of Tobit Drugs. Joe, who had served three terms as mayor, was a serious, hard-working man who had never had much interest in children. He had planned to earn money to support his family, and he expected his wife, Mary, would take care of all the child rearing. When little Paul was only five, however, his mother's life had been cut short by a guy working two jobs who had fallen asleep at the wheel.

Paul had only one clear memory of his mother. It was a cool afternoon in October. The fields were plowed down to mud, and it seemed like the earth stretched on forever. The sky was milky white. Paul's hand was stretched above his head, where his mother held it. She crouched down beside her son and pointed to the sky. The birds formed a seemingly endless parade of arrow-shaped formations.

"They're flying south for the winter," his mother said.

"Why?" he asked. He was at the age of "why."

"Well, it's warmer down there. Birds don't like the cold. So they go where it's warm, and then they come back in the spring."

"Why don't people fly south?"

"People have homes," his mother said. "People have places they belong. And when they find one place they belong, they stay there even if it's cold or rainy."

Each year, when the fall came and the birds began their southward trek so visible in the skies of Kansas, Paul liked to sit on the porch and think of his mother. As the years went by, the details of the woman faded: first the sound of her voice, her warm scent, then her expressions and the color of her hair. Eventually all Paul could remember with any clarity was the image of the birds and the arrow they formed across the sky.

There was a ceremony that took place after his mother died. It involved lots of baked goods and middle-aged church women whispering to his father, "How is he?" This is what happens when a church community adopts you. The minister and the Sunday-school teachers paid special attention to the boy, taking up the slack for his largely uninvolved father. The church became Paul's home. The minister was his surrogate father. Christ was his mother. Paul developed an uncommon ease with adults at an early age. History and tradition meant more to him than to most kids. He understood about past generations who now lived only in memory and ritual. In the universally awkward teen years, Paul retreated from his peers' world of sports, fashion, and dating. Paul liked to tell himself he was above all that. He had a higher calling.

In reality he was intimidated by the jocks, the trendy dressers, the budding rock stars, and the ones who partied and smoked. He couldn't even stand near the pretty girls without breaking out in a flop sweat. He assumed 90 percent of the girls were way, way out of his league. He loathed the good-looking bad boys they always seemed to choose.

Paul's response was to be anything but cool. If he wasn't walking down the hall, he had his nose buried in a book. He especially liked the Bible and Christian-themed novels—the meek were the heroes! He could hide behind them and pretend that he was not sitting with the popular kids because he was too busy reading to care. In the real world, he was always wondering if he'd stayed too long or left the room too soon. Books weren't like that. They were neatly divided into chapters, and his relationship with the characters ended amicably when there were no pages left to turn.

Paul spent his Saturday evenings working at his father's drug store in the hopes of earning Joe's interest and respect. He never truly felt he did. His favorite part of the job was chatting to the old people who came in to fill prescriptions. Many of them lived alone in old farmhouses, and the long journey to the store was their only real personal contact.

"I have a recording of the actual radio broadcast when the Hindenburg blew up. I think it's worth money, but I'd never sell it."

"I hear it's going to be a cold winter."

"My son is working for NASA now!"

It didn't matter what they said. It just mattered that they said it, and Paul was the friendly face. He knew intuitively that he didn't need to say anything clever or even to speak. He just had to smile, and they would ask for him when they came back. They made him feel useful and valued, something his classmates never did.

Studious Paul was always near the head of his class. He'd won awards and accolades for his volunteer work. He'd even been written up in the local newspaper several times. All this supported his belief that he was destined to do something important and meaningful with his life. Of course, back then success was easy. Up to that point he had always known the rules. If you wanted to get an A in class, the teacher told you exactly what to do. To win a local service award, there were straightforward guidelines. Paul had no nostalgia for homecoming parades, football games, or school plays, but he did miss his youthful certitude. As a professional minister, the rules would never again be as clear.

"INCOMPATIBLE"

In 1880, Baptist minister George Dana Boardman wrote a treatise called Studies in the Mountain Instruction. *"Ask yourself whether you are fulfilling Christ's condition of entrance (to heaven) or not," he wrote, "loving your enemies, doing good to those who hate you, blessing those who curse you…. It matters not what or how loud your profession is; how orthodox your creed; how often and devoutly you pray; how large your benevolences; how rapturous your closet experiences: all this goes for nothing unless you feel toward those who are hating and injuring you as Christ bids you feel. No criterion of piety can take the place of this test of the Mountain. There is no way of being a son of the Father in heaven except by doing as the Father in heaven does—even this, loving enemies, doing good to foes, sending sunshine on evil and on good, sending rain on just and on unjust."*

RELIGION WAS frequently a topic of the evening phone calls. Ian had a great curiosity about the Christianity Paul loved so much. He seemed to want to see the good in religion, but he had been burned. The church of his youth had damned him. Paul understood that Ian had abandoned religion for his own well-being. He never tried to push his faith on Ian, but he welcomed his questions, and he hoped it was something they might share one day. Perhaps God had given Paul an angelic vision in order to help Ian rediscover the divine nature of his own soul.

"Why are Christians so hung up about sex?" Ian asked one evening. "Mary was a virgin, Jesus was a virgin. Why is that so important? The world is sexual."

"Why is it important? Hmm… I guess because it helps to promote a stable society if people aren't so obsessed with sex. If they're not promiscuous. I think that's where it comes from."

"Is that what Jesus was about? Promoting stable society? I thought he was a guy who questioned the Pharisees and turned over the money-changers' tables and all that."

"He was. The *church* is about promoting a stable society. It's important, don't you think? Having a strong community."

"If I'm invited to the party."

"You are."

"I never understood why it's supposed to be less like animals to have sex only for procreation. I mean, isn't that exactly what animals do? They go into heat, they have sex, make new little animals, and go back about their business. That's being like animals. Being like a human is having sex because it feels good."

"I never thought of it that way."

"I mean, why should you have to justify giving someone pleasure? Shouldn't you have to justify giving someone pain? Like these people who go around bashing gays because they're good Christians—that's fine. That's good. But heaven forbid you give a guy an orgasm. That's evil."

"Why are you always arguing with me over things other people say? I'm not the representative for everyone who calls himself a Christian."

"I'm not arguing with you. I'm asking you why."

"But you're not asking me *my* opinion. You're asking me why different people think what they do."

"But in your church, aren't people expecting Christianity means certain things? They're not expecting you to get up and give a sermon praising fucking."

"I'm not antisex. I like sex."

"Me too."

"But I do think it should be in a committed relationship. I think you should love the person or at least have intimacy. I'm not talking about religion. I just think it's better for life. Don't you?"

"If you can find that. I haven't found that yet."

"That's hard to believe."

"I'm not exactly a catch."

"What are you talking about? You're crazy."

"Maybe."

"A one-night stand, maybe it's just me, but I think it's kind of self-indulgent."

"Have you done that? Had a one-night stand?"

"A couple times. It was fun in the moment, but afterwards it seemed pointless to me. You're not focusing on the other person, because you don't even know her. You're focusing on yourself. If you go around just having sex because it feels good to you—you're not connecting to anybody. You might as well be masturbating."

"I'd love to hear you say that in church."

"I'd word it differently."

"You'd kind of have to."

"My personal feeling about why the church tries to promote sex only within marriage is that ideally it preserves the real life-affirming kind of sexuality. It's not just about sensation and your own pleasure, it's about connecting to someone else on a deep and serious level. Maybe churches are clumsy in how they express that sometimes."

"Clumsy, like saying only straight people can have that."

"Yeah, clumsy like that."

"You don't believe that?"

"Believe what?"

"Leviticus 18:22."

"Oh, that again."

"You think two men can have 'life-affirming' sex?"

"Yeah, I do. Of course they can."

"Why? Don't you have the same Bible as everybody else?"

"I do. There are a lot of different translations, but putting that aside…. My Bible tells me, in the New Testament, that Jesus Christ came with a new covenant. That's why gentile men don't need to be circumcised to be Christians…."

"Are you?"

"Am I?"

"Circumcised."

"You're easily distracted."

"Sorry."

"You don't keep a kosher diet, right? You can mix cotton and linen. That's all Leviticus. It's the rules on how to be a good Jew. We keep the Old Testament to understand our tradition and heritage. To understand the context of Jesus's life and teaching. But no Christian follows all of the Jewish laws in the Old Testament, as far as I know. There may be some sect somewhere, but…."

"So it's only a sin for Jews to have gay sex?"

Paul laughed. "Well, I guess you could put it that way."

"Too bad for Abe Cohen," Ian said. "If the Bible says that, then why are so many churches antigay?"

"It's from culture and tradition. There's a lot of the Old Testament that's worth holding onto. Churches try to pass along the best of the traditions. So there's a lot of interpretation in that. There's nothing wrong with that."

"So what is that? Like, believe whatever you want?"

"No. Different churches have their own traditions. They're not just making it up as they go along. They've decided that certain things are important. The church where you grew up—they were very focused on the fight between good and evil, right? A struggle to avoid temptation and sin."

"Yeah."

"So that is their tradition, and they focus on passages of the Old Testament that support that tradition. This idea that you need to be vigilant all the time to avoid sin, it's always struck me as having an underlying idea that sin is appealing. That people naturally want to sin. I'm inclined to go the other way. I think people naturally want to be good, but life gets complicated and sometimes people make bad choices, hard choices."

"What's that got to do with sex?"

"Well, it's…. Most people don't want to kill anyone. I don't think most people want to harm other people. It's not a tempting kind of sin. So it helps support a tradition of a constant battle against sin if you focus on pleasurable things that are sinful. That's why those kinds of religions focus a lot on sex and abstinence. The more Evangelical churches tend to be more strongly opposed to homosexuality, premarital sex, that sort of thing. That's just my opinion, but I think that's why."

"What about *your* tradition? What does your church say about gays?"

"We're against discrimination, but we're not allowed to perform gay weddings, and the church won't ordain anyone who is openly gay."

"Why won't they ordain someone who's gay?"

Why wouldn't they? Paul didn't have a good answer. "I guess they think it's a bad example," he said.

"So it's, like, we want to be open and welcoming to you, even though we think you're a dirty sinner?"

Somehow the conversation was getting away from Paul. "I think our position is evolving," he said. "Society changes and the church changes too."

"But that's not what you believe," said Ian. "You don't think it's a sin."

"No."

"You think there's a new covenant. But your church says it's a sin, and you think that's okay because it's their tradition?"

"That's the position they took on the issue."

"And that's okay with you?"

Paul moved the phone from one ear to another, buying a moment to come up with a response. "I don't think it's a contradiction, theologically, for a church to take that position," he said.

"Well, it's a good thing you only have one toilet in the church-office bathroom, or you'd shit yourself trying to make up your mind which to sit on."

"What?"

"You're like a politician. You're talking out of both sides of your mouth. 'It's not, theologically, a contradiction'? If you think it's not a sin, and someone else says it is, then they're wrong. You can't just say, 'I don't think it's a sin, but if you do, hey, that's cool.' It is or it isn't. 'We want to be welcoming and open to you, but a gay minister would be a bad example.' What is that?"

"I don't think you're understanding what I'm saying."

"What do you preach on the subject—you personally?"

"I don't."

"Why not?"

"It never came up."

"It never came up? What is that? You just wait for things to come up? I thought you were the minister."

Paul was used to having the final say on questions of faith and religion. He wasn't expecting an argument from Ian, and it stung. He had been showing off, confident in his authority in this area. He wanted Ian to be impressed. Now Paul wanted to backtrack and reword his statements to make Ian understand what he meant. But he couldn't, because Ian had understood perfectly well. He saw right through it. Not only was Paul's position a bunch of contradictory mumbo jumbo, it revealed a flaw in his personality. Ian was right: Paul wanted to please everybody. It was one of the reasons his sermons had become so unmemorable. There was nothing remotely controversial in them. There was nothing to make people think in new ways. At least the fire and brimstone church of Ian's youth had had some fire.

"Are you still there?" Ian asked.

"Yeah, I'm still here. I'm just thinking."

"I'm sorry. It's just a sensitive subject for me."

"I'm… I'm not a hypocrite."

"I didn't say you were."

"I think you just did."

"No, I don't think you're a hypocrite."

"I represent the church," Paul said, trying not to sound hurt, "but I don't agree with all of their positions on the issue. You're right. The church would like to have it both ways and make everyone comfortable. I think they're going the right way, affirming that we shouldn't discriminate and trying to encourage an open dialogue. But I'm not talking out of both sides of my mouth. I'm just trying to explain what I think, and what the church says. That's all."

"I get that," Ian said. "I really wasn't saying you're a hypocrite."

"It's a relationship with a church, like a friendship. You don't stop speaking because you disagree on something. Say I'm a Republican and you're a Democrat. I'm not going to say 'Let's call the whole thing off.'"

"You're a Republican?"

"Uh-oh. Maybe we should leave the politics for another night?"

"Sounds like a good idea."

When they had finished their conversation, Paul went to his computer and looked up everything the church council had written on the issue of homosexuality. It was all well wordsmithed by some committee, designed to please everyone and offend no one. The more he read, the less clear he was on what it was trying to say. There were long passages discussing official openness to gays, laying out a commitment to nondiscrimination based on sexual orientation. Churches were to actively welcome gay members and also to understand that homosexuality made many people uncomfortable. They were not to do anything that could be perceived as "promoting a gay lifestyle," and yet they were not to do anything that might promote homophobia. They were to welcome openly gay couples, yet not perform any kind of ceremony to acknowledge a same-sex union. In all this tightrope walking, one thing was unclear—how was a member of the faith supposed to *feel* about gays? Was a gay relationship a sacred union or a sinful aberration? Were gays just like us in every way, or was there something wrong with them?

The only thing unequivocal in the literature was this: the church would not tolerate an openly gay minister. After a preamble about the "frailties of the human condition" and the "pressures of society" that ministers faced, it stated clearly: "Practice of homosexuality is incompatible with Christian teaching."

Reading the passage sent chills down Paul's spine. "Incompatible with Christian teaching." They were words he had never tripped over before. He must have read the material in the past, and it had seemed reasonable enough to him at the time. Now he was taking it all personally—and he was afraid. The church had always been his life. Who would he be if the church rejected him? Who would he be if he was not a minister?

"Frailty." Wasn't that a strange way to describe risking everything in the name of love?

"Incompatible with Christian teaching." That was the most revealing passage of all. With all the kind language about the "mysteries of human sexuality" and homosexuals being "equally deserving of God's love," it all came down to this. A gay relationship was not a blessed union of souls. That was why there could be no weddings. It was a "frailty of the human condition," a sinful act, a weakness to be tolerated out of compassion, though "incompatible with Christian teaching."

The next morning, Paul picked Ian up at his apartment as usual. The morning sun illuminated Ian's face with a warm glow. His beauty made Paul especially nervous. Ian apologized again for the argument on the telephone.

"Don't apologize," Paul said. "You should say what you think. Anyway, you were right."

"I don't know," Ian said. "I think maybe you were right about not expecting a church to be perfect. People aren't perfect, right? A church is just people."

In his office that day, Paul wrote a sermon about his disagreement with the church's statement on homosexuality. It was truly inspired, passionate and soaring in places. The main theme was that no one was beyond Christ's love and that the union of any two souls was truly blessed. After several hours writing and revising and then reading and rereading, Paul was sure it was perfect. Then he deleted the document. He knew he would never be brave enough to deliver it.

PRETTY

"Now this sculpture by streams, or by gradual weathering, is the finishing work by which Nature brings her mountain forms into the state in which she intends us generally to observe and love them. The violent convulsion or disruption by which she first raises and separates the masses may frequently be intended to produce impressions of terror rather than of beauty; but the laws which are in constant operation on all noble and enduring scenery, must assuredly be intended to produce results grateful to men."

—*John Ruskin,* Modern Painters, Volume IV

ONE OF the benefits of talking with Ian on the telephone was that Paul could not see his face. Freed from the distraction of his beauty, Paul was able to be himself. *What must that be like*, he wondered, *to be beautiful—to have that just be a fact about you—you're left-handed, you're tall, you're beautiful.* When Ian looked in the mirror in the morning, an objectively attractive face looked back. It was a question, of course, that would be laughable to speak out loud. "What is it like to be beautiful?" But it remained an undercurrent in Paul's thoughts—an issue calling out to be addressed.

Finally, one night they were in their respective homes, each watching the movie *Titanic* while discussing the action over the telephone. Paul had the subtitles on and the volume on mute. He was lying on his side on the futon as he held the phone to his free ear.

"You see the priest there, praying with the people on the deck?" Ian asked. "That's you, right? I mean, that would be you if you were on the *Titanic*. You'd be praying with people."

"Sure," Paul said as he propped himself up on his elbow to get a better view of the set. "What else could you do? It would be good to have something you could do."

"I wouldn't be anybody," Ian said sounding a little petulant. "I'd be, like, a random steerage passenger."

"Nothing wrong with that."

"I wouldn't have anything to do but drown."

"Well, I think the priest drowns too," Paul said. "Leonardo DiCaprio is a steerage passenger. He's the star of the film."

"I wouldn't be the star. I'd be one of those guys running around with the rats."

"You could be the star. You have the leading-man looks."

"God, I don't have leading-man looks."

He couldn't possibly believe he was ugly. "You do have a mirror in your house, right?" Paul asked.

"George Clooney has leading-man looks," Ian said. "Me, I'm just…."

"What?"

"Well, 'pretty' is always the word that people use."

Well, of course, Paul thought. It was the right word. The softness and the delicate vulnerability of Ian's face ignited the same protective instincts he'd felt when attracted to a woman. But it was not the feminine aspects that excited Paul. Prettiness in a woman was perfectly ordinary, expected, and therefore not intriguing. It was the combination of the delicate prettiness with a masculine energy—his angular shapes, the deep voice, his confident stance: yin and yang in one form. Masculine prettiness fascinated.

"That's not bad, is it?" Paul asked.

"Not if you're a little girl."

"They probably mean it as a compliment."

"It's not very serious. Handsome is serious. Pretty means 'Well, he's nice to look at, but I think I'll have a conversation with someone else.'"

"They wouldn't say that if they knew you."

"The kids at school would laugh and say, 'Are you a boy or a girl?'"

"Kids always tease you about something. There are worse things you could have been picked on for than being too good-looking."

"What did they tease you for?"

"Me? Everything. You wouldn't know it now because I'm such a trendsetter, but I was a total nerd in school."

"Were you the teacher's pet?"

"No, just a nerd. I'd sit in the back of the room and sneak peeks at the Bible during class. That's what kind of nerd I was."

"That is pretty nerdy, Paul. But kind of cute. They were teasing me for being a fag."

"Don't use that word," Paul said, sitting up. "I don't like it."

"It's the truth."

"But I don't like that word. I don't like it when black people call themselves 'niggers' either."

"You like 'queer' better?"

Paul shook his head. "Come on, they weren't teasing you for that," he said. "They couldn't possibly have known that. You couldn't have known that yet."

"I knew."

"Really? As a kid in school?"

"I think I always knew."

"I'm sure the kids didn't. That can't be what they meant. You're not feminine. You're just...."

"Pretty?"

"Yeah... but I mean it as a compliment."

"Okay. Thanks."

"No one would know if you didn't tell them. The girls must have been crazy about you in high school," Paul said.

"I guess so. My friends were always girls. They weren't *girlfriends*, though."

"You never had a girlfriend?" Paul asked.

"Nope. Not interesting."

"I thought you'd have tried it at least once," Paul said.

"You think I'd change my mind?"

Sensing they had moved on from *Titanic*, Paul picked up the remote and turned off the television. "No," he said. "I just thought you'd have tried it."

"Have you tried it?"

"What do you mean? Yeah, I had girlfriends," Paul said, setting the remote back down.

"No," Ian said, "the other direction. With a man."

"Oh. No."

"Never thought about it?"

"Ah, thought about it...." Paul fumbled. "Well, thinking, that's... um...." Paul couldn't find the right words. Since he met Ian, he thought about it all the time—and that was the one thing he couldn't share with him.

"I'm sorry," Ian said. "I made you uncomfortable."

"It's okay," Paul said, pulling himself together. "Yes. I've thought about it."

"Ah," Ian said with a laugh. "Minister's true confessions." Paul could see Ian's raised eyebrows all the way through the phone line. "You've never told anyone that before, have you?" Ian asked.

"No."

"What did you think?" Ian asked. His tone was flirtatious.

"What?"

"When you thought about it, what did you think?"

"I'm not telling you that."

"Okay."

"Maybe we could change the subject."

"Okay. What made you decide to become a minister?"

"That is a change of subject!"

"Guinness Book!"

"Why I'm a minister…." Paul got up and started to pace. "Well, when I was in school, I found Christ, and it meant a lot to me. It became the most important thing in my life, and I wanted to share that and make other people feel that way."

"You found Christ?"

"Yeah."

"That's… I mean…."

"What?"

"I just, I don't know what that means, 'finding Christ.'"

"It means allowing Jesus into your heart."

"I still don't know what that means."

Paul ran the fingers of his free hand over his forehead, as though he could dislodge the right words from his brain by massage. "It means accepting that you are loved as you are, whoever you are. You are worthy of love and Jesus loves you."

"Jesus loves me."

"Yeah."

"But…."

"What?"

"No, nothing. That's cool."

"But what?"

"Well, I mean… so what? I mean, what good does that do? Jesus can't hold you in his arms. You can't call him when your car breaks down. He's like the ultimate unattainable man."

The ultimate unattainable man. Paul liked that. He wondered if he could somehow use it in a sermon.

"He can't hold you in his arms," Paul said, trying his best to avoid using a *preacher* tone, "but sometimes people have trouble finding that in life. Even if you have someone who *can* hold you in their arms, maybe they're distracted with stress about their own problems. They just can't always be what you need. Jesus is always there. When everyone else is unreachable, he never goes away."

"So it's like a fantasy romance," Ian said. *A romance with Jesus*—now there was Paul's sermon topic.

"I've seen it make a real difference in people's lives," Paul said. "When people know they're loved, they don't treat one another as badly."

"Hmm."

"You're not convinced."

"No."

"Why?"

"If that's the way it works in your church, then that's great," Ian said. "I know you believe what you're saying. But a lot of people talk about finding Jesus and accepting Christ as their savior and then go around bashing other people."

"You can't blame Christianity for the things some people do in its name."

"Why not? They give Christianity the credit. Why shouldn't I give it the blame?"

"Because…. Why? Because it's not for them," Paul said. "It's for you, because I think you're missing out. There's a whole spiritual, religious dimension of life. You shouldn't let other people's attitudes rob you of that. It's important. You're like… you know what you're like? You're like a guy who's had his heart broken who vows never to love anybody again. That doesn't hurt anybody but himself."

"So you're saying Jesus broke my heart, but I should give him another chance."

"That's basically what I'm saying. It sounds like you had a bad breakup. But you can love again."

"You seem like a hell of a minister, Paul."

"That's a unique way to put it."

"I'll tell you what. Just for you, I'll try it. I'm going to come to the service and listen on Sunday. Maybe I'll be convinced."

SUNDAY

There is hardly a religion in the world that doesn't hold some mountain as sacred. To the Native Americans of the region, Mount Rainier, or Tahoma, as they called her, was a goddess. Mount Meru, according to Hindus, sits at the center of the world between Heaven and Earth. The Tibetan peak Kailas is said to be the home of Shiva, Lord of the World. Muhammad met the angel Gabriel and received the word of God on Mount Hira. Japan's Mount Fuji is a site of pilgrimage for three hundred thousand Shintos a year. Zeus ruled from Mount Olympus. The Mongols buried their leaders in high places. The Babylonians called their temples "Mount of the House," "Mount of the Storms," and "House of the Mountain of All the Lands."

PAUL SPENT extra time on that Sunday's service. He wrote and revised and practiced reading it in front of the mirror—something he had not done since he was a young minister just starting out. He stopped at each line and imagined Ian's reaction. The sermon topic was "A Romance with Jesus." It was both inspired by, and written for, Paul's audience of one.

That Sunday, Paul sat at the front of the congregation in his black robe with the Bible in his lap. When it came to worship, Paul was usually a King James man. Even though it was in some respects one of the least accurate translations, it was the Bible of his youth. The poetry of passages was so musical and familiar that Paul could not imagine any other language having the same effect—transporting the congregation from the mundane, everyday world into the spirit of worship.

Emily started to play the prelude on the small church organ. Paul watched as the church members filed in, dressed in their Sunday best—skirts, dresses, shirts and ties. He smiled and nodded at the familiar faces as they took their favorite places in the pews. He glanced toward the back of the room, over their heads. Ian did not come in. The Bible moved up and down as Paul's right leg started to bounce. He craned his neck trying to see beyond the sanctuary doors into the lobby. Ian was not there.

The prelude ended. Paul stood and lit two candles. He did it slowly, stalling for as long as he could. Then, when he had paused as long as humanly possible, he delivered the call to worship:

"Make a joyful noise unto the LORD, all ye lands. Serve the LORD with gladness: come before His presence with singing. Know ye that the LORD He is God: it is He that hath made us, and not we ourselves; we are His people, and the sheep of His pasture. Enter into His gates with thanksgiving, and into His courts with praise: be thankful unto Him, and bless His name. For the LORD is good; His mercy is everlasting; and His truth endureth to all generations."

As Joanne Johnson delivered the announcements, Paul sat, crestfallen, with a pleasant Sunday expression frozen on his face. Emily waved her arms, and the choir stood in unison.

"Jesus, lover of my soul," they sang. "Let me to Thy bosom fly, While the nearer waters roll, While the tempest still is high: Hide me, O my Savior, hide, Till the storm of life is past; Safe into the haven guide; O receive my soul at last!"

That was when Paul saw Ian's slim figure sneaking into a pew in the back. He was wearing a blue T-shirt with a rock-band logo and jeans with a hole in the knee. As the people around him shared hymnals and sang off-key, Ian shuffled from side to side. His right arm was straight, and he held the elbow with his left hand. To Paul, it was as though the entire congregation had become part of a black-and-white movie and only Ian was in vivid Technicolor.

There was a special music in Paul's voice that day, expressing all the divine wonder and appreciation that called him to the ministry. Paul truly felt the presence of God with him. Ian slipped out the back of the sanctuary during the moment of silence to go back to his normal Sunday custodial chores.

When the service had finished, Paul received many compliments from the congregants who shook his hand as they filed out of the sanctuary. But he was anxious for only one opinion: that of the custodian.

After Paul and Ian had wrapped up their respective church duties, they met in the parking lot so Paul could drive Ian home.

"How did you like the sermon?" Paul asked.

Ian's eyes turned heavenward. He nodded, still lost in his own thoughts. He spoke in a soft voice. "I really liked it."

Ian snuck into the service again the following Sunday, just after the opening prayer and before the opening hymn. He picked up a hymnal and followed the words with his eyes but did not sing. He stood again for the scripture reading but did not recite. During the sermon, he sat forward and listened intently. Again he slipped out during the moment of silence. The following week, Ian was in the sanctuary to hear Emily play the prelude. He stood with the congregation and sang the opening hymn. He recited the responsive reading. He stayed through the sermon. He passed the plate along during the offertory and held hands with the neighbors to either side of him during the closing benediction. Two Sundays later, he arrived early and sat in a pew in the very center of the congregation. When the offertory plate was passed, he put a dollar in.

Paul felt a sense of mission and purpose he had not felt for years. Watching Ian returning to worship, Paul felt truly "called." His ministry took on a new energy. The sermons were inspired and unique. Everything in life was taking on a new color, and Paul's new enthusiasm for life spilled over into everything he did, the way he spoke to people, the care he took with every meeting. He could now feel congregants' joys as deeply as he had previously felt their sorrows. People walked away from a meeting with the minister feeling revived and passed that along to each other. Attendance was growing.

For the past several years, social outreach and projects had continued on their own momentum, but very few new ones had ever gotten off the ground. It was not that Paul had actively discouraged them, but when people came to him with their ideas, he never followed up. He'd vaguely encourage them and leave it to them to take care of the details. Most of the ideas were dropped. Now every new idea seemed to have promise. If a church member suggested visiting a homeless shelter or teaching an evening cooking class, Paul immediately got Julie to put a date on the calendar, get a notice in the newsletter, and made sure it happened. Almost nothing worth trying was dropped. The sense that things were happening at the church built on itself.

Someone Like You

"In every-day matters, how wonderfully the divine law of creation is obeyed! for mountains have been tunneled, rocks have been cleft in twain... the earth has been lacerated, scourged, cut, and hallowed, till, tired of the treatment or forced to submit, it has paid its ransom in coal, gold, silver, iron, lead, copper, and in other valuable, attractive, and important minerals.... It was easy enough to plunge into the earth, disturbing its equanimity, and making it disgorge its treasures; but it was not so easy for us to plunge into ourselves, finding the precious minerals in our own brain or heart, and knowing the value of our God-given natures."
—*Rev. Caleb Bradlee Davis*, Sermons for All Sects, *1854*

PAUL AND Ian spoke on the phone almost every night now. They spoke frequently of love in a general way, always dancing around the edges of the real question: whether or not they could love each other.

"Julie was telling me about your wife, Sara. It sounds like she was really popular."

"She was. She was the one everyone loved. They just let me preach a sermon now and then."

"How long were you married?"

"Eleven years."

"Wow," Ian said. Eleven years seemed like a brief moment to Paul. Yet, he realized, it must sound like an eternity to Ian. It was nearly half of his young life.

"How did you meet?" Ian asked.

"At the church," Paul said with a nostalgic smile. "When I came here to be the minister, it was my first church. I'd been an assistant minister, but I was young and new to the area. I didn't know anyone or how they did things. The guy who was here before me, he had been the minister for more than twenty years, and everyone loved him. So he was a tough act to follow, and I was really nervous. I had no idea what I was doing. Everyone said, 'You should talk to Sara.' 'Ask Sara.' She was just the center of everything. So I had to go to her. She convinced me I could do the job and that the people would accept me. Then, well, she became the center of everything for me. And when I married her, it was like I married the whole church."

"So was that what you loved about her?"

"It was part of it," Paul said. "The reason everyone loved her was that she was so full of energy and outgoing." Paul suddenly realized how much Ian and Sara had in common. Outwardly they seemed like completely different people. Sara was straitlaced. Ian was rough around the edges. But they had that same spark of life, the same energy.

"I'm always attracted to extroverts," Paul told Ian, "outgoing people. I really need someone like that to balance me. I never have any idea what someone like that sees in me, though."

"She must have thought you were smart and deep," Ian said. "You probably made her think."

"Maybe," Paul said. He gazed at one of the many wall-mounted photos of his wife, seeing it as if for the first time. The image of her smile still filled him with a sense of comfort and peace. "I just fell for her right away. I think the main thing that worked about our marriage was that she understood me. It's hard to put it any differently than that. She sometimes knew what I was thinking before I thought it. We were completely connected. When she was sick, she was always trying to comfort me." In spite of his best efforts to control his emotions, Paul felt tears welling in his eyes and a tightness in his throat. "She was the sick one," he said, "and she was trying to make *me* feel better. That's the kind of person she was."

"That must have been hard," Ian said.

"It was hard." Paul wiped away a tear. "We had so many plans together. That's the worst part. She was only thirty-four. We wanted to have kids, but we put it off, and then she got sick. I still miss her. I miss talking to her."

"You're lucky, though, that you had that," Ian said. "That's real love. I wish I had something like that.... I wish I could meet someone like you."

Paul snapped back to the present. "Like me?"

"Yeah. Someone devoted like that. Someone really there for you. Who knows me better than anybody. Deep, connected."

"Well, you already know someone exactly like me."

"I know but, I meant…. Wait, what do you mean?"

"Nothing. I just mean… I didn't mean anything."

"Are you sure?"

"You've really never been in love?"

There was a pause as Ian decided whether to allow Paul's abrupt change of subject. "Not really," he finally said. "I thought I was once, but it wasn't, really."

"What happened?"

Ian seemed reluctant to talk about it. "He cheated on me," he said. "A lot. He acted like it was my fault. He said I was… 'needy' was the word he used. 'You're pretty, but you're too needy for me.'" (Paul was finally getting comfortable with the pronoun "he" when Ian talked about love.)

"You don't seem needy to me," Paul said.

"And you would know," Ian said with a laugh, "because you bailed me out of jail and put me into rehab."

"Exactly."

"Then there was the guy, my first 'love.' You know, the first one I slept with. I thought I was in love with him too. He was older."

"How much older?"

"Not a lot older. Like five years, but I was only sixteen."

"He was twenty-one years old?"

"Let me check your math, sixteen plus five… yeah, that's right."

"What kind of twenty-one-year-old sleeps with a high school kid?"

"A selfish one, I guess. Someone who wanted to be adored. He was a dancer. Really sexy."

"Did he know you were sixteen?"

"Oh yeah. He used to call in to school for me. You know, like, 'This is Ian's father, he won't be in school today because he has the flu.'"

"That didn't seem… wrong to you?"

"It was exciting," Ian said. He was clearly enjoying the memory—or shocking Paul. It was hard to tell which. "I couldn't believe someone like that would be interested in me," Ian continued. "He'd take me to parties with all these dancers and actors. We'd get drunk together. He liked cocktails, mixed drinks. He taught me to mix martinis, Tom Collins, Long Island ice tea."

"So he was a good influence all around."

"He taught me valuable life skills."

"I hate this guy."

Ian laughed. "I was head over heels for him. 'This is the one,' you know? Happily ever after."

"Happily ever after at sixteen?"

"What did I know?"

"You're a romantic."

"I was."

"Not anymore?"

"I don't know. I'm smarter. Sometimes I wish I could still just completely fall head over heels like a teenager, you know? I still like the idea that maybe there's this one right guy. That it can last forever. Like soul mates. Is that… I don't know. Kind of sappy?"

"No. I don't think so. I believe in soul mates."

"So you're a romantic too."

"What happened with the dancer?"

"Oh, he got a job with a ballet company in Texas and went away. I sent him these e-mails, like, 'I love you,' 'I miss you,' 'I think about you all the time'—pretty much every day, but he never wrote back. Then finally, on my birthday, I called him. I couldn't wait to hear his voice. He was just completely cold. He said, 'You're not relevant to my life anymore. You should cool it with the e-mail.'"

"Wow, that's…. Wow."

"Yeah."

"Well, it's his loss."

"Uh-huh. They always say that."

"You're only twenty-four. I can't believe how much you've experienced."

"I haven't experienced anything. Nothing worth experiencing, anyway. What about you? Do you think you'll fall in love again?"

"You know, I couldn't imagine myself loving anyone else for a long time. But now, I'm starting to feel like I'm ready. I think I could fall in love again."

"Happily ever after?"

"Maybe, with the right person."

HOLY COMMUNION

In 1916, the historian and critic John Charles Van Dyke wrote a book devoted to the meaning of mountains. "How often that feeling in the presence of the great elements has expressed itself in a mist of tears and a choking in the throat!" he wrote. "The high-blown pride of the human breaks under him just here. His reason deserts him and the religion of the Garden comes back to him. There in the high mountains, which were God's first temples more truly than the groves, he forgets to pray for himself, but has rapturous praise for the Power that planned and the Hand that wrought. He is back to a primitive faith from which he never should have wandered."

PAUL HELD out the silver tray with the little cups full of grape juice and the plate with bite-sized chunks of Selma Mead's home-baked bread. The parishioners inched up the aisle, each silently taking a sample, then turning and circling back to the pews. As the members in the middle pews filed into the aisle, Ian stood and walked with them, two places in line behind Frank the usher.

"Take and eat this in remembrance of me.... Take and drink this in remembrance of me."

Paul focused on the motion, the words, the ritual, but his eyes kept darting back to Ian. He felt a tangible sensation in the center of his abdomen that grew stronger every inch Ian came closer to the altar.

"Take and eat this in remembrance of me.... Take and drink this in remembrance of me."

Maybe the Catholics had it right after all. Paul might have been holding a tray with bread crumbs and cups of juice, but the objects were transformed. They had not become lumps of flesh or goblets of blood, but they were no longer what they had been. They had a meaning in the church, in the context of the service, that they did not have outside those walls or outside the moment. It was a meaning that could not be articulated, only experienced. There was the collective meaning, the history, the union of the community, and there were meanings that no one but each individual could know.

"Take and eat this in remembrance of me…. Take and drink this in remembrance of me."

The word "holy" goes back before Christ. It is related to the word "holistic" and the word "whole" and means "that which is inviolate, intact, complete." To feel holy is to feel whole. In his ministry, Paul had felt moments of awe and reverence; he had felt satisfaction and pride; he had felt stimulated intellectually and moved by the music and poetry. But he could count on one hand the moments when he truly felt holy—when all the energies of his life aligned, his ego slipped away, and he felt the Lord working through him.

Only two people now stood between the minister and Ian. Paul felt his hands begin to tremble.

"Take and eat this in remembrance of me…. Take and drink this in remembrance of me."

It was a communion just like any other in a Protestant church on a given Sunday. The ritual was performed over and over again. For a minister, communion was a repeated experience, mundane and commonplace. Yet today it was singular, an experience fully shared by only two.

Ian had lived disconnected, outside of society, out of touch with his soul. He was a man eclipsed by his body. How many men had tried and failed in a vain attempt to possess his physical beauty? The skin, which marks the boundary between the self and the nonself, can be touched and caressed, but physical consummation doesn't transfer beauty from one to another. It remains a property of only one. Had the men blamed *him* when they didn't get what they wanted?

Somehow Ian had come to believe he was a pretty package with nothing worthwhile inside. By taking communion, he was acknowledging the divine nature of his immortal soul. His inner and outer beauty merged and became one, inviolate, complete. Of course, a person's soul can never truly be possessed either. But unlike physical beauty, it can be shared: a pair of souls in holy, holy communion.

Ian stood before him. His eyes (in this light they were blue) tilted toward heaven. Paul dropped his normal cadence. He paused, took a deep breath, and said, more slowly than usual: "Take and eat this in remembrance of me."

Ian took a piece of the bread and put it in his mouth.

"Take and drink this in remembrance of me."

Ian took a drink from the small cup. Then he turned right and circled back to his pew with the others. The entire exchange had taken only seconds, yet the moment felt so big, it was almost infinite. Paul was humbled and small.

Maybe all of it, the angelic vision, the fascination, the desire—maybe he had found its purpose. Maybe it all led up to this moment.

A Dormant Volcano

The serene, peaceful face of Mount Rainier disguises the fact that it is actually the most dangerous volcano in America. We try not to tell you too much about that when you're actually on the tour—but we'll have a video for you later. We've titled it "Things We Don't Want to Tell You Until You Get Away from the Mountain."

You don't see any lava flows right now because the volcano is dormant. "Dormant" means it's taking a nap. It is not dead, just sleeping. Molten lava can't be contained forever. It will happen one day. Rainier will come down. One thing you don't need to worry too much about, though, is a sudden explosion. Geologists say the mountain isn't going to so much explode as it will fall to pieces. The seemingly solid foundation will crack and fall apart, burying the surrounding population in soot and ash. Enjoy your stay!

SERGEANT TIM Goddard of the local police force was a longtime member of Hope Church and considered its minister to be like part of the family. Like everyone in the church, he knew Ian. He knew about his history, that Ian had agreed to go to rehabilitation and to abstain from drinking as a term of his plea bargain for a DUI. He also knew about Paul's special project to help the kid turn his life around. So when he looked out the window of his cruiser on a Wednesday evening and saw Ian wandering along the side of a busy road, clearly drunk, instead of turning right and taking him to the police station, Tim turned left and brought Ian to the church. He knew the church building would be open because his wife, Jenny, participated in Paul's Bible-study class before her choir rehearsal, which usually ran until 9:00 p.m.

Bible-study class was finished, and Paul was checking e-mail when he heard a rap on the sliding window of the locked outer office. He got up, walked to Julie's desk, and spotted Tim in his police uniform with his hand on the shoulder of a hunched Ian.

"Damn it, Ian!" he muttered under his breath. He unlocked the outer office door and let Tim bring Ian in. Ian turned his head and looked down over his left shoulder, away from Paul.

"I'm sorry to bother you, Paul," Tim said. "I found him wandering along Harbor Street. I thought he might get himself hurt. He blew a .19. I didn't want to violate him. I know you've been helping him out."

"It looks like I haven't been doing a very good job of it," Paul said, glaring at the side of Ian's face. He sighed and then turned to Tim. "Thanks for bringing him here. I really appreciate it."

"No problem," he said. "Hope you can sort it out."

Tim closed the outer office door behind him when he left. Ian turned his head slowly to the right, still tilted down. He raised only his eyes to Paul and flashed his best injured-faun expression. Paul was having none of it. He raised his hands as though he might strangle the young man.

"What were you thinking?" he nearly shouted. He turned his back on Ian and walked into his own office. Ian followed and closed the inner office door behind him.

"I wanted to see you," he said. "So I walked."

"And you happened to stop by a distillery on the way?"

"That's funny!"

"How did you even know I'd be here?" Paul asked. "It's almost 9:00 p.m."

"You have that thingy on Wednesdays."

"You could have called and I would have picked you up."

"I wanted to surprise you."

"Well, congratulations. I'm surprised. How much have you had to drink?"

"Don't be mad."

"Why shouldn't I be?"

"'Lead us not into temptation,' right? That's fine for you because you're not tempted by anything."

"How do you know what I'm tempted by?"

The edges of Ian's lips curled slightly upward. His hair tumbled onto his flushed cheek as he tilted his face down. He bit his lower lip and then looked up with only his sea-green eyes. He opened his mouth as though he were about to speak but instead bit his lip again and gazed back down at the floor.

Paul rubbed his index finger and thumb over his eyes until they came together at the bridge of his nose. He waited, but Ian did not say anything. "What were you about to say?"

"What are you tempted by?"

"Don't do that."

"I'm not doing anything."

"Yes, you are."

"You're the one who said it. Tell me. Tell me what you're tempted by."

"No."

"Why should I listen to you, then?" He inched closer to Paul, leading, as always, with his hips.

"You're drunk."

He shook his head. "Doesn't change anything."

"Go home and come back when you're sober."

"What if I don't come back?"

Paul felt a brief, involuntary moment of panic. "What?"

"What if I don't come back?"

"You will."

"What if I don't?"

"Well, I hope you will."

"Why?"

"I'm not having this conversation with you tonight."

"When? When are you going to have this conversation with me?"

"I'm not. Go home."

"You're so scared." Ian came in closer, so close that Paul could feel the warmth of his body. Ian laid his hand on Paul's cheek, parted his lips with his own, and invaded his mouth with his tongue. He tasted like whiskey.

Paul pushed him away. "Stop it! I'm not doing this with you. Not like this."

"Like this?"

"I'm not having a drunken fuck with you so you can forget it ever happened."

"Wow. They let ministers say 'fuck'?"

"There's a special exception. It kicks in when you're talking about having sex in a church office with a guy who also happens to be half your age and shitfaced." He shouted the last two words.

"You're mad."

"You think?"

Paul sat down at his desk and laid his forehead on his hands with the palms pressing into his eyes. Ian stood, chewing on his thumbnail.

Without looking up, Paul said, "Why do you have to make things so ugly? Why are you always playing with me?"

"I wasn't playing with you."

"Please just go home."

Ian started to walk out the door, then stopped and turned back. "Hey, um, Paul?"

Paul looked up.

Ian was biting his lip. "I, uh, can't go home. I can't drive."

Paul set his jaw. He jumped up from the desk and led Ian roughly by the elbow. They reached the lobby as the choir was filing out.

"Could someone drive this one home?" Paul asked the crowd as he released Ian's elbow. Without waiting for an answer, he went back to his office and slammed the door. He hunched at the desk, his cheekbones resting on this thumbs, his hands in a steeple position, supporting his forehead. He sat there until he was sure all the people had gone.

The following day, Paul asked Julie to pick Ian up for work. When he arrived, Ian knocked on Paul's door and peeked in. His hair was pulled back, and he was wearing the same Pillsbury Doughboy T-shirt he'd had on the first day they met. His eyes were nervous and sad. "Paul?" he said.

Paul was angry at him, angry at his perfect cheekbones, his soft lips, the eyes that changed color from green to blue. He was angry with him for looking like an angel and for refusing to be one. He resented the way Ian filled him with desire. Most of all, he was angry at Ian for making him confront his own instincts and passions.

They'd been through too much together now. It was way too late for it to be an "experience" or an "encounter." Whether he was ready to admit it or not, Paul knew in his soul that they were already in love. If he took the leap and made love to Ian, it would be profoundly real.

What would that make him? Paul would become a "gay man." Maybe for the rest of his life. He couldn't change his identity that easily.

"I don't have time to talk to you today," he said. "I'm very busy."

"But, Paul, we have to talk about this."

"Not today," Paul said. "I'm very busy. Shut the door behind you."

Ian pressed his lips together, then turned and walked out the door. Paul ate lunch at his desk with the door closed.

In the afternoon, Ian tried one more time to talk to Paul in his office.

"Not here," he said. "I don't want to have this conversation here."

"I'll call you tonight, then?" Ian asked. Paul didn't answer.

He had Julie drive Ian home.

PAUL'S CHOICE

Back in 1870, two white men asked a Nisqually to guide them to the top of Mount Rainier. He took them as far as the snowline and then refused to go farther. He warned the climbers of the physical dangers, the storms, the winds, the avalanches, and above all, the summit spirits. Even today, many Nisqually believe the snowline separates the sacred from the profane, and they will not cross it.

THAT EVENING Paul sat in front of the television letting CNN news wash over him. The caller ID displayed on his television set: "Ian Finnerty" and the phone number. Three times the number appeared, and three times Paul let it ring out and go to voice mail. The red light on the phone on the end table flashed. He could see it out of the corner of his eye as he watched TV. He knew he couldn't avoid Ian forever, but he was not ready to talk to him yet. He wanted the whole thing to just go away. He had become comfortable with the situation, desiring Ian, growing closer every day, coming close to the line and never crossing it.

Getting to know Ian and to care about him was innocent. So was enjoying the pure aesthetic pleasure of Ian's beauty. Helping him get back to sobriety, giving him a job, being a friend—all of that could even be considered admirable, elevated. His own secret desires didn't change any of that—as long as he didn't act on them.

What was it about sex? Why did it seem so important? It was just the touch of certain body parts. How could that have such significance that obsessions could be ignited, marriages could be destroyed, and careers ruined? It shouldn't matter so much. Yet some friendships could never feel complete without it.

His desire for Ian had the force of an ocean, a tornado, or a mountain. The mountain defies any effort by humans to tame it. You can build at its foot if you like, but when the mudslide comes, you'll be buried regardless of ordinances or zoning laws. None of that exists in the face of nature. Nature has its own order. There is no motive to ascribe to the mountain. It does not kill with vengeance or purpose. It just evolves as it does, and whatever human order we try to create is temporary at best. If sexuality was a force of nature, then wasn't that closer to God than the human laws we try to impose on it?

Ian and Paul had gone as far as they could as friends. It was clear to Paul that they both felt the magnetic pull of an attraction that could not be denied. It was time for Paul to make a choice. His only options now were to say yes or to say no. Either choice would change things forever. If he said no, the flirtation and the hour-long phone calls would stop, and Ian would slowly but surely drift away. The idea of going on without Ian in his life was inconceivable and painful. Saying yes was even more daunting. An affair with Ian had the power to undo him. He might be risking everything he had and didn't know what he would gain. The perfect untouched dream would be replaced with an uncontrollable reality that would transform Paul's life in all kinds of messy but maybe beautiful ways.

After a few hours staring at the flashing red light on his telephone, curiosity got the better of him. He picked up the phone and punched in the code to retrieve his voice mail. Although Ian had called three times, there were only two messages.

"Paul, it's me," the first message began. "I'd really like to talk to you. Can you please call me back?" Paul pushed the 7 key and deleted the message.

"It's me again," the second message said. "I know you're there, Paul. I'm sorry about how I acted last night. We really need to talk about what happened. I'm going to call again in a half hour. Please pick up this time."

Paul had just pushed the 7 a second time when he heard a car pull up out front. He went over to the window and looked out. It was a silver sedan with the words "E-Z Taxi" painted on the side.

"Shit!" It seemed Ian had gotten tired of waiting for Paul to pick up the phone.

Paul went and stood behind the door. He knew Ian was coming, and normally he would have opened it, but he waited for the knock, buying some time. He took a deep breath before he turned the knob.

"Hi," Ian said. His hair was down now. He stood with his hands on his hips. His expression was no longer nervous and apologetic but confrontational.

"I didn't know you were coming," Paul said. "You should have called first."

Ian raised his eyebrows. They both knew very well that Ian had called, many times, and that Paul had not picked up. Paul looked away, an admission.

"Are you going to let me in?" Ian asked.

Paul gestured toward the living room, and Ian stepped inside.

"We have to talk about this," Ian said.

"I don't understand you. You were doing so well. After everything you went through, the shakes, the detox, you want to start all over again?"

"I'm sorry I let you down."

"Don't apologize to me. You let yourself down."

"Yeah, I did. But it happens. Alcoholics have relapses. And you know that…. That's not why you're avoiding me."

Paul folded his arms across his chest with his right hand resting on his left shoulder, protecting his heart. He was facing Ian's general direction but could not look him in the eye.

"You were drunk," he said. "Can't we leave it at that?"

"You weren't."

Paul looked down at his feet and didn't answer.

"I'm sorry that I was drinking," Ian said. "That was a mistake. But I'm not sorry I kissed you."

He waited for Paul's answer, but it didn't come. He tilted his head sideways, trying to make eye contact, "Are you?"

Still no answer.

"You said I was playing with you," Ian went on. "You're the one playing with me. Tell me if it's all in my head. Maybe I'm crazy. But last night, it didn't sound like you were saying no…. Was I wrong?"

Paul did not look up.

"I'm not playing with you. I really… have feelings for you," Ian went on. "You're just… you're not like anyone I've met before. I had an ugly life before I met you. The guys I was with, they didn't care what happened to me. They didn't see me at all. But you're different. The way we talk for hours. You're probably the smartest person I know. And you listen to me. And you were just there for me. No one's ever done anything like that. And I feel like…. But if I'm reading it wrong, you have to tell me. Just tell me and I'll put it out of my mind. I can do that."

Paul looked at Ian, knowing he should say something, but he could not answer. He turned his gaze back to the carpet.

"You probably should have run away screaming by now," Ian said. "I would understand if you did…. I know I'm not…. Maybe I'm just imagining things because I want them to be there. But I don't think I'm crazy…. Yesterday I decided I had to find out. But I was so nervous. I thought I'd just have one little drink. I thought maybe I could do that. But I can't. It was stupid. I know I fucked everything up…. I don't know what I'm saying…."

Ian had taken every risk. He had trusted a stranger at his most vulnerable. He had made the first phone call. He had risked rejection and made the first move. Now he was standing before Paul emotionally naked.

For the first time, Paul truly understood that when Ian looked in the mirror in the morning, he didn't see a beauty—he saw someone covered in scars. Paul was ashamed. He did not deserve Ian's admiration. He'd been as blind as all the others to anything but Ian's beauty. He'd wanted to hang him on a gallery wall and look at him like a work of art, an object. Paul wanted everything in life to be pretty. He was so focused on outside images: Ian's beauty, what people would think. What did any of that matter? Ian was brave, and Paul was a coward. He was denying a deep human connection and trying to make his own fear into a virtue.

"Help me, Paul," Ian pleaded. "Can't you say anything?"

Paul looked Ian straight in the eye. "You're not crazy."

Ian sat down on the futon, the same one he had slept on the night Paul brought him home from jail. He was smiling. "I knew I wasn't," he said to himself. To Paul he said, "So what are we going to do?"

Paul sat down beside him. He wanted to protect Ian, to erase all the wrong that had been done to him, and to keep it from ever happening again. A strand of hair had fallen across Ian's face. Paul reached over and tucked it back behind his ear. Then, with his thumb, he traced the line of Ian's cheekbone, and then the line of his lower lip.

"My angel," he said.

He leaned in and allowed his lips to nearly brush Ian's. He hesitated and leaned back enough to allow Ian's face to come into focus. His eyes were full of expectation, his soft lips slightly parted. Paul leaned in again, and this time their lips touched, tentatively at first. Ian responded, gently teasing Paul's lips with his own. An invitation and an answer. It was natural—the first time and yet not the first time—because this moment had been practiced so often in fantasy. Yet the fantasies were no preparation. Paul's imagination hadn't the talent to get it right. He'd focused on the lips and the tongue and the building sense of arousal. But he'd neglected to include all of the senses and all of the emotions. He'd failed to include the sense of smell, the musky, smoky scent of Ian. He'd failed to imagine the twinge of fear and anxiety and the open space it created inside when he let it go. He'd failed to fully include his sense of hearing, the small short breaths and long sighs so close to his ear. He'd focused too much on his mind and his thoughts, which he now released completely. They got lost in each other, lost in the dance. Paul ran his fingers through Ian's hair. He felt Ian's hands exploring his back and shoulders. For a moment he seemed to disappear into pure sensation and emotion.

He was startled when he heard words; his intellect was hardly prepared. "Should we go to your room?" Ian asked. Without waiting for Paul's answer, he stood up and put out his hand. "Come on," he said.

Paul didn't move.

"Don't worry," Ian said. "I promise I'll remember it in the morning."

Paul smiled. Then he stood up and took Ian's hand.

After months of anticipation, Paul would have liked to have made love with a passionate fire or to have melted into Ian so fully that they did not know where one ended and the other began. The sex was clumsy, uncoordinated, and inelegant, but it didn't matter. They touched each other, they embraced and they laughed, and Paul sensed that it was one of the most intimate experiences either of them had had in a long time.

WE

These days we tend to think of snowcapped mountains as peaceful, spiritual places. The serene spot where the Earth meets Heaven, a fitting home for angels. In earlier times, though, sinister beings populated the high peaks. Trolls, flying dragons, and witches were all said to live in the mountains.

In 1555, a Swiss naturalist named Conrad Gesner sought to prove that there were no monsters. He climbed Mount Pilatus to confront the ghost of Pontius Pilate, which was said to haunt Lake Pilatus. Gesner and a friend tossed stones into the waters of the lake, a deliberate provocation. The earth did not tremble; the skies did not erupt with thunder and lightning; there was no cataclysm of any kind. After that, Westerners began to release their fears about monsters on the mountains.

PAUL WOKE up first. He felt warm and relaxed as he watched Ian sleep. He was on his side, facing Paul, with the sheets down around his waist. All the anxiety and worry were gone. He had made his choice, and there was no turning back. He reached out and gently touched Ian's face, tracing a light path along his cheekbone. Ian twitched, as though a fly had landed on him. His eyes opened. When he saw Paul looking back at him, Ian smiled.

"Hi," he whispered.

"Hi," Paul whispered back. "Are you hungry? I have eggs, bacon, oatmeal. I might have some yogurt."

"Do you have Lucky Charms?"

"Lucky Charms?"

"I like the little marshmallows."

Paul laughed. Somehow he never imagined in his life he'd be in bed with a naked man talking about sugared cereal.

"I don't have Lucky Charms," he said. "But I'll stop today and buy some. For next time."

"Next time?" Ian gave his curlicue grin. What an amazing, amazing smile. "You're pretty sure of yourself."

"Well, I have to keep practicing until I get it right," Paul said.

"How about right now?" Ian wrapped an arm around Paul's waist.

"Right now we have to get up and go to work," he said, peeling Ian's arm off him.

Mentioning the church brought the larger world into focus. Nothing had changed, and yet everything had changed. He was going to ride to work with Ian like he always did. But today he would be walking in to the church with his lover—his young, male lover.

"We… we can't tell anyone about this," Paul said.

"Duh!" was Ian's reply.

"You have a way with words," Paul said, because he was too scared to utter the thought that had first flashed across his brain: "I love you."

He got out of bed. Lying next to Ian, he imagined himself to be very sexy. When he walked past the full-length mirror, he was shocked and disappointed to see his same old self. He stopped and scowled at his doughy midsection, the white hair at his temples and on his body, the first signs of crow's-feet and lines on his forehead.

"Nightmare," he said.

Ian came up behind him and put his arms around Paul's waist. The two were now standing, naked, framed in the mirror with their faces beside one another. "Beauty and the beast," Paul said.

"Don't call me a beast!" Ian said.

"That's good," said Paul. "You're full of shit, but that was good." He raised his hand with the palm up and waved it back and forth to underline each of their faces in the mirror. "What is wrong with this picture?" he asked.

"Nothing," Ian said. He kissed Paul on the neck. "Absolutely nothing."

From then on, Paul and Ian were hardly ever apart. Paul found excuses to run into Ian in the hall at church, and they would stop and talk. They ate together in the lunchroom. After work, they would go to eat at a restaurant or straight to Paul's place for dinner. When they had finished eating, they'd unfold the futon and curl up together to watch movies on TV. Paul let Ian have control of the remote, and he chose films Paul would never have watched normally. He was fond of science fiction, especially older science fiction, and karate movies. Everything he liked was "the best."

"*They Live!* This is the best— have you seen it? We have to watch this! Oh my God. The original *Invasion of the Body Snatchers*. This is the best!" Paul didn't particularly like the movies, but the fact that Ian enjoyed them made them fascinating. They usually didn't make it to the end of the film, anyway, before they were making love.

In the morning, they stopped by Ian's apartment to get him a change of clothes, and the routine would start again.

Sara had never been all that interested in sex. Paul had been able to persuade her a few times a month. He had the impression that it was only something she was willing to do because she liked the way he held her afterward. She insisted that each of them shower before making love. On good nights, it drew out the suspense and anticipation, but for the most part, it turned their sex life into a ritual rather than a spontaneous expression of desire. She always wanted the lights off, as if she thought God was watching with disapproval and in the dark she might be able to hide. Her block against uttering dirty words was total. That language marked the boundary between being a lady and a whore. As much as he tried to reassure her that he would think no less of her, it was an inhibition they could not overcome. He could beg, plead, and cajole her to tell him what she wanted, but the most she could manage was a pained and tearful, "I want you."

Now everything was reversed. Ian's desire seemed to have no off switch. He wanted sex in the morning, in the shower before work, before the dinner plates had been cleared from the table. Paul didn't have that level of energy. He couldn't quite convince Ian that there was a real difference between being forty-two and twenty-four.

"I'm an old man, you know," Paul would say.

"You're not old," Ian would answer.

"Tell me how you feel when you're forty."

Ian would tilt his head down, the better to show off his puppy-dog eyes, wrinkle his nose slightly, and in a boyish tone he'd plead, "Please, fuck me?"

If he had asked Paul for a pony using that expression, he probably would have bought him one. Paul wished he had been born a little bit later so he and Ian could have been young at the same time.

Ian was a good lover, more concerned with Paul's pleasure than his own. As Paul became more comfortable and familiar with Ian, and his level of trust grew, he could sometimes let himself give way to pure experience. At those moments, he did not think about the mechanics of sex, his performance, or love, or even Ian. Ian was no longer in his thoughts but in his arms, in his mouth, on his skin. No longer a being but a set of sensations, and he was aware of Ian experiencing him in the same way. They disappeared into touches, scents, flavors, beating hearts, and coursing blood. It didn't happen every time, but when it did, it was transcendent. And when Ian came back into focus, his angelic face flushed and serene, Paul ached with the depth of the connection he felt for this singular other being and no one else.

One afternoon, about three weeks after their first night together, Paul was in the sanctuary going over some of the music for the service with Emily, who was seated at the piano. Paul stood at the altar beneath the suspended cross with the afternoon sun forming lines on the red carpet at his feet. Ian was vacuuming just outside the door in the pavilion. When Emily had finished, she left the room. Paul stayed behind, making a few notes on his papers. Ian turned off the vacuum and walked up to Paul. He glanced around quickly to make sure no one was watching, and then he leaned in and whispered in Paul's ear. He told Paul exactly what he wanted to do to him that night, complete with vivid adjectives and all manner of four-letter words. It was the most filthy, pornographic, and delicious thing Paul had ever heard. He swallowed hard.

Ian backed up a step and tilted his head down as he maintained eye contact. This made his eyes seem larger and made his face appear its most childlike and innocent. Then he turned quickly and went back to his vacuum as if nothing had happened.

The contrast between the sacred and the profane—the shocking setting, right under the cross; the angelic face and the obscene language— the danger of being discovered, and the delayed gratification were a powerful cocktail. The anticipation on the drive home was so strong that Paul could barely make it through the front door before tearing off Ian's clothes.

The next morning Paul made the "offhand" comment that it was kind of inconvenient to keep driving Ian back and forth from his old apartment.

"Yeah. It kind of is," Ian said.

Paul let it drop.

The next day he mentioned again how inconvenient the drive was, adding, "We should try to come up with a solution."

Ian agreed, but Paul let it drop again.

The next day Paul added a new suggestion: "Why don't you just come stay at my place?"

Ian agreed immediately.

It was the easiest moving day he'd ever been involved in. Paul arrived in the morning to find Ian already waiting outside, sitting on the stoop and smoking a cigarette. He was wearing his plaid slacks and matching jacket with a deerstalker hat that would have made a middle-aged man look dowdy. On Ian it was a fashion statement—hip and sexy in its utter goofiness. When an ordinary-looking person wears an ugly hat, you assume he is out of touch with fashion. When a young and beautiful person wears an ugly hat, you assume you're the one who doesn't get it. All Ian's worldly possessions fit into a worn green backpack he had slung over his right shoulder. In his right hand, Ian held the fly-eating plant. Paul was struck once again by how young Ian was and how even younger he looked. To anyone watching, Paul might have appeared to be a dad picking up his high school son for school.

The passion had propelled Paul so swiftly that it only now dawned on him what a huge step he was taking. Inviting Ian to move in with him was probably the biggest risk he'd taken in his life.

What am I doing? he wondered. Then Ian smiled, and the thought drifted away.

Ian's clothes took up only one drawer. Sometimes Paul would peek at the foreign objects in Ian's drawer, delighting in what their presence represented. He would pick up a pair of Ian's jeans and wonder at the narrowness of the waist. He grinned at the unfamiliar rock-band logos on the well-worn T-shirts. They were a symbol of Ian's youth—his "otherness."

The extra shaving kit in the bathroom pleased him, too, but it didn't intrigue him the way Sara's toiletries had when they had first moved in together. She had all those mysterious feminine lotions and potions. They were a wonderful symbol of her "otherness"—"a woman lives here!" During the months when they were first married, he probably spent hours gazing at small bottles and tubes, contemplating their contents.

Ian never bothered to close the bathroom door. Whether he was cleaning his ears with cotton swabs, poking at a zit on his forehead, or sitting on the toilet, he was completely unselfconscious. It was the sort of thing Paul would normally consider to be a distasteful breach of etiquette. For some reason, with Ian, he didn't mind. The difference in their attitudes about privacy simply fascinated Paul, who couldn't even brush his teeth in front of anybody. Ian was, in the best way, shameless, a physical being free from shame about his incarnation.

Their domestic life soon took on a comfortable routine. That was what Paul cherished the most—not the moments of excitement and sexual ecstasy, but the ordinary day-to-day stuff, the things that would never make it into photo albums or journals. The monotonously recurring events were the very substance of life, and it was precious to Paul to be living them with his angel.

Paul would watch Ian bringing in the mail, add an item to the shopping list, or take out the trash. Paul did most of the cleaning, because Ian couldn't be bothered. Ian put the dishes in the dishwasher, because he liked that, but he didn't like putting them away. Paul did that. Ian liked throwing clothes in the laundry but not taking them out of the dryer and folding them. Ian never got near the toilet with a brush. He liked vacuuming, but the vacuum usually didn't quite make it back into the closet when he'd finished. He seemed to have a general block about putting things away, and away was where Paul liked things to be.

But Ian had an unfair advantage. He could get out of just about any household task he didn't want to do with a flirtatious glance or a pout. Paul could put up no resistance to that face, and God help him, Ian knew it. Paul was vaguely aware that he was setting a precedent he might regret when the initial infatuation wore off, but he was powerless to do anything about it. It was probably karma, anyway. When Paul married Sara, he left all the household chores to her by default. She took them on without comment or complaint, and he never thought to question it.

Even though Paul disapproved of Ian's smoking, he secretly enjoyed the cigarette smell—which permeated everything—and the saucers placed around the house to be used as ashtrays, even when they spilled and left gray ash on the tables and carpets. They were tangible, physical reminders of the presence of his lover and of how his life had changed.

Ian's main job was household chef. While he cooked he would often listen to music through headphones and sing along. Paul didn't know most of the songs, but he was fairly sure Ian sang them all off-key. It was an endearing flaw, like the small gap in his teeth. Ian liked to toss little scraps of meat into the fly-eating plant, which he kept on the kitchen windowsill.

He had an adventurous palate. He loved anything spicy and liked to experiment with flavors. If he ever encountered an unfamiliar fruit or vegetable at the store, he had to buy it to see how it tasted. Paul was the opposite. The only spices he liked were salt and pepper, and he didn't have any interest in trying anything more foreign than french toast. Ian made it his mission to sneak a little variety into Paul's diet.

"What is this?" Paul would say as he pushed something around on his plate with his fork.

"It's couscous."

"What's that?"

"It's fine. It's wheat. Just try it."

"What's that on top if it?"

"They're called vegetables."

Paul picked the chickpeas off with his fork and put them to one side of the plate.

"You're not eating those?"

"I don't like them."

"Have you tried them?"

"I don't know. Can I… make a peanut butter sandwich?"

"No. I made this for you." Ian rolled his eyes. "I can't believe you're older than me."

Paul had forgotten all the simple pleasures of being part of a "we:" sleeping like spoons, telling your dreams to someone when you woke up, being comfortable around someone before you'd combed your hair, communicating completely with half sentences and facial expressions, the joy of not having to do or say anything.

He was constantly inspired by Ian—his spontaneity, his playfulness, and his unique outlook on life. Yet it was still his beauty that completely engaged his imagination. Paul loved Ian because he was beautiful, and Ian was beautiful to Paul because he loved him. He did not know which came first or where one stopped and the other began.

Sara had been beautiful to Paul, but not a true beauty. She would never have been confused for a runway model. Ian could be. (A "male model," people always say, because beauty is a woman's job and male beauty an aberration.) Paul felt like the popular kid in school for the first time. There was only one problem: he couldn't tell anybody.

Sara had been his girlfriend, then his fiancée and his wife. Everyone knew about their status. To the world Ian was nothing more than his employee or a student. No one would have any reason not to go after him and steal him away. Paul had reacted so strongly to Ian's beauty that he could not imagine anyone—male or female—feeling any differently. Paul still found it hard to believe that someone so attractive could possibly fall for someone like him. One day Ian would wake up and realize his error too. When he did, there would be fifty guys waiting. Paul saw predators everywhere.

Women of all ages instinctively flirted with Ian. Paul didn't mind that. It wasn't a threat. The real problem was the men. Whenever Ian smiled at a male church member or shook his hand, Paul watched for extended glances and meaningful laughter, and he saw them everywhere. It didn't matter if Paul knew the man to be straight, happily married with five kids. A nod and a grin became a seduction, a mere prelude to a passionate embrace, an invitation to a bedroom or a dark corner.

During the week, the church was a predominantly female environment, and Paul was comfortable as Ian roamed around the building, doing his work. It created no anxiety. On Sundays, however, he found it hard to let Ian out of his sight. He stood in the doorways and around the corner from the rooms Ian cleaned. If a conversation with a man during coffee hour went on a bit too long, Paul would approach and tell Ian there was a bathroom somewhere that desperately needed immediate cleaning. He was a guard dog, circling, monitoring. He had never been so driven to distraction by jealous impulses before. It made him feel out of control, and he hated it.

THE LUNCHROOM

One of the most famous mountain aphorisms is that "the only Zen you find at the tops of mountains is the Zen you take up there." Another way to put it is, "That which you are seeking is causing you to seek." It was the lesson Dorothy learned in Oz (at the top of an enchanted mountain where she melted the Wicked Witch). The corollary is that unless they are surprised out of their complacency, people generally see exactly what they expect to see and no more. A mountain could stand right in front of them, and they might never know it was there.

THE SPONTANEITY and lack of pretense that so inspired Paul also drove him crazy at times. Ian was social and talkative and a complete open book. He loved to chat with the girls in the office, especially with Julie. Paul had not hidden the fact that Ian had moved in with him. The staff, and eventually the entire congregation, knew. But Paul hoped he could preserve the illusion that Paul and Ian were a bit like a father and an adopted son.

But nothing could stop Ian from talking about his life with Paul and the things they did together. When Julie talked about her husband or Emily about her boyfriend, Ian would jump in with, "Paul does that too," or "I can never get Paul to try anything new," or "Paul snores like a steam engine." Paul was just waiting for the day when he would casually mention which side of the bed he slept on.

Fortunately, he had one secret weapon—Ian's face. The women in the office were all so infatuated with Ian that they were entirely blinded to the seemingly obvious fact that when talk turned to boyfriends, Ian immediately thought about the minister. They simply never made the connection.

One day in late December, as the staff was getting ready for lunch, Ian came in from shoveling the church walkways. His nose and cheeks were red. He sniffled and jumped up and down to get the circulation moving.

"It's freezing out there," he said.

"You poor thing!" Marlee said. "Do you want some hot chocolate? We have some mix in the religious education office closet."

"Thank you," he said.

As Marlee heated the hot chocolate in the microwave, Julie brought Ian a box of tissues.

"Be careful you don't get sick. There's a flu going around," Julie said.

"Here," said Emily, "I'll hang up your coat."

Paul stood at his regular place at the back of the table. He opened a paper sack and took out the pair of sandwiches Ian had packed for them that morning. He placed one at Ian's regular spot then sat down to watch the privately amusing spectacle of the women flirting with and babying his lover.

Emily handed the mug of hot chocolate to Ian. He sat down, cradled it in his hands, and let the steam warm his face.

Paul unwrapped his sandwich, lifted the upper slice of bread, and eyed the ingredients with suspicion.

"Why do you put this stuff on my sandwich?" he asked Ian.

Ian rolled his eyes. "Take the avocados off. I'll eat them." To Julie he said, "It's no fun cooking for him because he doesn't like anything."

"Are you saying I'm boring?" Paul asked.

"Yeah," Ian said. "But in a good way."

"There's a good way?"

"It's endearing. It's cute."

Julie and Marlee laughed. Paul smiled, but he hoped Ian could read his subtext, which was: "I might have to kill you if you call me cute in front of people again."

Ian put the warm mug against his cheek.

"You're still cold?" Emily asked. "Look at you, your ears are still bright red."

Ian rubbed his ears to warm them. His hair flipped back behind his shoulders, uncovering the left side of his neck.

Emily squinted at the exposed skin.

"What is that on your neck?" she asked.

Paul felt the blood rush to his cheeks, and he hoped the women in the room would not notice his blushing.

"It's a hickey!" Marlee said. "He has a hickey on his neck!"

Ian put his hand over the side of his neck and instinctively turned to Paul. "I do?" he asked. Paul nodded. (Subtext: "Yeah, sorry.")

"I didn't know that," Ian said, still looking at Paul. (Subtext: "Why didn't you tell me there was a hickey on my neck before I left the house?")

"You have a new girlfriend?" Julie leaned forward, her eyes wide.

"What's her name?" asked Emily. "You should bring her here so we can meet her."

"Yes, we want to meet her!" Julie said.

"I… I don't have a new girlfriend," Ian said.

"We won't tell anybody," Emily said. "Is it somebody in the church?"

"It's… it's not like that," he said. "I don't have a girlfriend."

"How'd you get the hickey, then?" Marlee asked.

Ian turned to Paul again, his face pleading for a rescue.

"Come on," Paul said to the women. "He obviously doesn't want to talk about it. It's none of our business."

Talk then turned to holiday plans, what relatives people were visiting, who was doing the cooking, how much everyone had to get done before Christmas, and how unlikely any of them were to actually get it done in time.

"I still have no idea what I'm getting Jim," Julie said. "He's so hard to shop for. He doesn't collect anything. He doesn't have any hobbies. I have no idea what he wants."

"I know what I want to get Paul," Ian said. "I have it all picked out in my head. Is anyone going to the mall soon? Maybe someone could give me a ride?"

"I can take you," Julie said. "I have to go anyway. What about tomorrow after work?"

"Great! I'll buy you dinner," Ian said. "Do you like Mexican? There's a place near the mall that has the best margaritas anywhere."

"Margaritas?" There was a little scold in Paul's voice.

"Just because I can't drink them doesn't mean she can't," Ian said. "I have all this hard-earned knowledge. I need to put it to some use. I wish I could figure out how to make a living at it. It's the only thing I'm an expert in."

"That can't be true," Emily said.

"It's not," Paul said. "I've been trying to convince him to go back to school. I'd help you."

"You should," Julie said.

"I don't know," Ian said. "Maybe. I'd have to know what I want to do first."

"Actually," Julie said, "maybe you can help me with my New Year's party. Maybe you know where the best prices are on wine and stuff."

"Stuff? You mean booze?" Ian asked.

"Yeah," Julie said with a laugh.

"I'm your man," he said. "It's good to be able to use my powers for good instead of evil." He took a bite out of his sandwich. The surplus avocado slices tumbled out onto the table.

"If you happened to want to bring the new girlfriend that you don't have, you're both invited to the party," Julie said.

"Um, thanks," Ian said, picking up the avocado and trying to fit it back in the sandwich. "Since she doesn't exist, I probably won't bring her, though."

After lunch, Julie stopped in Paul's office. She looked back and forth as though someone might be listening.

"So, what does she look like?" she asked.

"What does who look like?" Paul asked.

"Ian's new girlfriend."

"I don't know," he said.

"You must have seen her. Ian's living in your house and he doesn't drive, so she must have to come to pick him up."

"I haven't seen her."

"Men." Julie shook her head. "You are so unobservant. You don't notice anything."

Paul pressed his lips together to avoid laughing.

TINSEL

In his 1858 discourse On Beauty, *the Scottish man of letters John Stuart Blackie wrote about the sublime landscape of the mountain. "The silver thread of the wandering waterfall, the nodding plumes of the solitary birch tree, the gleam of light through the dark rocky chasm, the pleasant murmur of the lonely mountain river, the smoke upwreathing from the solitary shielding—all these are points of pure beauty, which calm and soothe the soul amid what is called the 'savage grandeur' of the scene. Were it purely savage, it would be pleasing only to a savage mind, and to a diseased imagination, to which mere horror and terror had become necessary stimulants.... Even the tempered sublime, in fact, cannot be the habitual atmosphere of a healthy human life. It is beauty that must be our daily food: sublimity only our occasional banquet. Therefore, when any object naturally sublime is constantly presented to our eye, it is so enrobed in beauty, that the feeling of awe, with which it might otherwise overwhelm us, is moderated into love."*

THE FOLLOWING evening, Ian returned from his shopping excursion with Julie lugging three bags and a four-foot Christmas tree. He set the tree down in the middle of the living room floor and then dashed into the bedroom. Paul could hear him hiding something in his drawer. He came back out singing "Winter Wonderland"—off-key, of course.

Ian set the shopping bags down on the coffee table in front of the futon and removed the contents, throwing the plastic bags and receipts to the side as he went. He produced three holiday music CDs, two boxes of candy canes wrapped in plastic, an artificial pine Christmas wreath, a long holly garland, and two boxes of silver tinsel in strands.

"Here's my favorite," Ian said. He pulled out a sprig of mistletoe with white plastic berries attached to a piece of white cardboard with a twist tie. He held it over his head and waited for his kiss.

Paul complied. Still standing face-to-face, with his hand on Ian's hip, he said, "I can't believe you bought all this stuff."

"Isn't it great?" Ian picked up one of the CDs, unwrapped it, and dropped the plastic on the floor. He put it in the CD player and pressed play. Paul was surprised that he had chosen Bing Crosby and not some modern rock band. Ian hummed "White Christmas" with Bing and started moving furniture around to create just the right spot for his little Christmas tree.

Paul was looking at the pile of packaging. "You're going to clean this up, right?" he asked.

"Yes, Mom," Ian said. He had placed the tree on the end table in front of the window and was now opening a box of tinsel.

"I don't really like tinsel," Paul said. "It gets all over the house."

Ian pulled a handful of tinsel from the package and tossed it into Paul's hair. "Bah! Humbug!" he said.

"Stop that!" Paul said, brushing it off. "Are you planning to vacuum up the stray tinsel, or am I going to end up doing that?"

"This isn't as fun as I was picturing it," Ian said, pouting. "You're not in the Christmas spirit."

Paul sighed. "You're making that face."

"Yeah, I know," Ian said, raising his eyebrows. "Is it working?"

"Yes." He sighed again. "But I have a box of ornaments somewhere. In the garage, I think. If I can find them, can we use them instead of the tinsel?"

"Okay. You look for the ornaments, and I'll put up the wreath."

Paul went into the garage and dug through boxes of storage. He had essentially stopped celebrating Christmas when Sara died. They had never made that big a deal of the holidays at his house as a kid, and the marital merrymaking had been all Sara's. She couldn't get enough of Christmas and started decorating around Halloween. While they were together, he had found her enthusiasm for the holiday infectious, but when he was on his own, the season became lonesome and melancholy.

Christmas was a work day for him, a busy time, and that made it bearable. He gave the services so other families could celebrate. He took what pleasure he could from their faces. Then he went home and watched TV. It seemed foolish to put up decorations for himself. He opened the presents that came in the mail when they arrived, and there was no need for holiday music for that.

Now that he would have someone to celebrate with again, Christmas suddenly did seem fun. Paul found the box of ornaments buried under some old tax receipts. He went back into the house humming "White Christmas." Paul pushed the pile of plastic bags aside and set the ornament box on the coffee table. When he opened it, he was surprised by the power of the emotion. He had not seen the ornaments since he and Sara had packed them up their last Christmas together. The box had become a time capsule.

Each ornament in the box represented some part of their lives together. Paul could see Sara, her thin hair covered by a head scarf, taking the fragile ornaments down from the tree and wrapping them in paper towels. Right on top was an ornament Paul had forgotten entirely because it had hung on the tree only once. It was a crystal angel blowing a golden horn.

"She'll watch over you," Sara said when he opened it. They both understood the unspoken second half of the sentence: "After I'm gone."

She put it on the tree that day, up at the top near the star. A few days later, Paul packed the decorations away, along with the angel ornament, and purposely put it out of his mind. It had remained in the box unseen and unremembered until now. Paul brushed a tear away from the corner of his eye.

"What is it?" Ian asked.

"I'm sorry," Paul said. "I didn't expect…. Sara gave this to me our last Christmas together. I forgot about it."

"I'm sorry," Ian said. He put his arms around Paul and let him sink onto his shoulder. They held onto each other silently for a full minute. Paul finally let go.

Ian took the angel from Paul's hand and held it up to the light. "It's really beautiful."

"It's supposed to be Sara's angel watching over me. We knew that Christmas that…." He brushed away another tear. "I didn't mean to spoil the mood."

"It's okay," Ian said. He handed the ornament back to Paul. "You should put it on the tree."

"I don't know," Paul said. He wrapped the angel back up in her paper towel. "Why don't we put up the other ones, and I'll think about this one."

Ian picked up an ornament shaped like a country church with a steeple. "Is this the church?" he asked.

"It's supposed to be." Sara had given that one to Paul their first Christmas together, when they were still dating.

Paul unwrapped an ornament in the shape of a house. He had gotten that one for Sara to commemorate buying their home. His first mortgage. Now *that* was a commitment!

Ian was hanging a God's eye made of sticks and yarn. Sara had made that with the kids in her Sunday school class. He placed it next to a glass hummingbird, a gift for Sara, who took childlike delight in the birds in their new yard. Every ornament in the box was constructed around a memory of Sara. Ian, unaware of their meanings, happily arranged and rearranged them on the tree until he was satisfied with the color and symmetry. He backed up and stood beside Paul, gazing at his work.

"It looks good, doesn't it?" he said. "You know what would make it better, though?"

"Tinsel?"

"Tinsel!"

"No."

When all the decorating was done, Paul, of course, scooped up all the packaging and deposited it in the kitchen trash. He made some hot chocolate, and he and Ian sat on the futon admiring the festiveness of the room. This entertained them for a good six minutes. So they unfolded the futon, pulled out the afghan, and curled up to watch whatever was on TV. Ian rested his head on Paul's right shoulder with his arm draped across Paul's chest. Paul lazily ran the fingers of his right hand through Ian's hair. A commercial for engagement rings came on: "A diamond is forever."

"Did you buy Sara a ring like that?" Ian asked.

"Yeah. Not quite that big, but… I have it. Do you want to see it?" Before Ian could answer, Paul rolled off the futon and headed into the bedroom. When he returned he was holding a small box, shiny cardboard. He sat back down beside Ian, removed the lid, and handed the box to him. The gesture called to mind a marriage proposal. Realizing this, Paul spoke quickly to break the spell. "That's her ring."

It was silver with a modest stone in a square setting. Sara's fingers had been small—the ring looked as though it might fit on Ian's pinky—but he didn't try it on. He ran his finger slowly over it and then handed it back to Paul.

"They gave it back to me when she died," he said. "I wanted to be there with her, holding her hand. That's how I pictured it. But it took a long time. She really held on. There was a week where we were just waiting, thinking she would go at any time. So I went home to sleep one night, and almost as soon as I got home, they called and said I should come back. By the time I got there, she was gone. The nurse said 'I'm sorry' and gave me this."

"That's rough," Ian said. Paul closed the box and set it on the end table under the Christmas tree.

"How did you know you wanted to marry her?" Ian asked.

"She knew before me. She kept dropping little hints." Paul's eyes gazed heavenward, and he smiled at the images in his own mind.

"So it was her idea?"

"I just needed a little nudge."

"How did you propose? Was it romantic?"

"It was supposed to be," Paul said, laughing. "I took her on a picnic, right by the lake. And I had wine and candles. But there was too much wind, and the paper plates kept flying away and the food got dumped on the ground, and the candles wouldn't stay lit. But I asked her anyway. She said yes."

Ian was gazing to a spot on the wall just beside the television at a picture frame that displayed one of Paul's favorite images of Sara from their wedding day. Beside the photo, in the same frame, was a poem in calligraphy, composed and hand-lettered by a church member. The topic was being reunited in heaven.

"Do you think Sara is waiting for you in Heaven?" Ian asked.

Paul followed Ian's gaze to the photo. "I think she is," he said.

"I wonder if I'll go to Heaven."

"Of course you will," Paul said, kissing him on the forehead.

"So we'll all be there together."

"I guess so."

"Do you think she'll be jealous?"

"Hmm. I don't think there's jealousy in Heaven. Do you?"

"I don't know. You're the minister."

"We talked about it, you know. Just before she died, when she was so sick. She said she wanted me to meet someone and fall in love again."

"Have you… fallen in love again?"

"Head over heels."

"I… I'm in love with you too."

The next day, Paul visited Sara's stone at the cemetery. He brushed off the snow, then rubbed his hands together for warmth.

"I've met someone," he told her. "I know he's probably not what you expected. He's not what I expected. But I really think you'd like him. He's had a hard life, and I have no idea how he managed to turn out the way he did. He could be bitter and angry, but he sees the best in people. He's trusting. He has so much faith in me. Oh, but he's messed up all my habits. It drives me crazy sometimes. He can't make a bed. He leaves his underwear on the floor. But I think I needed to have my habits messed up. You know that. So if he messes up the house too, well…."

He stood, rubbing his red nose and wishing she could answer.

"He's beautiful inside and out, but he doesn't know it," he said with a chuckle. "Well, actually, he knows about the outside. He definitely knows about that, but it's like he's always thought that was all he has. He doesn't know how beautiful he is as a person. God blessed me that I can see it. I don't know how it happened. But I love him. I don't know what it means, or what's going to happen. I thought I knew who I was…. I wish that I could talk to you about this. I think you'd understand."

Then an idea came into his mind. It was so clear and sudden that he had to believe it had come from outside—directly from Sara. Somehow she had found a way to speak to him.

"Let me go."

That evening Paul packed away most of Sara's photos, leaving only the wedding picture with its poem about heaven on the wall. Then he took all the ornaments down from the tree, hanging only the crystal angel on a branch near the top.

"What are you doing?" Ian asked. "I put a lot of work into that. I had it just right."

"I thought we could go out and pick out a few ornaments together. Something that represents us, not me and Sara."

Ian put a hand on the side of Paul's face. Using only his eyes, he said, "I love you."

"You know what else I think this tree needs?" Paul asked.

"What?"

"Tinsel. Lots of tinsel."

HAPPY NEW YEAR

To many, mountains are no more than an impediment to progress. They block our will, interfere with our movement and migration. Not far from Donegal, Pennsylvania, in a quiet region of dense spruce forest, lies a little-known three-mile tract of overgrown and cracking highway that has hardly seen a tire since 1968. The road heads toward the face of Laurel Hill and stops short at a stone arch with a rusted overhang, its opening blocked by a white corrugated-metal door partially obscured by a massive pile of road salt. There is little sound but the distant rushing of the traffic from the Turnpike that has been routed away from it, stranding the portal in time.

This is the Laurel Hill Tunnel, a remarkable feature of the original Pennsylvania Turnpike, known in its day as the "Dream Highway." The ambitious interstate, which cut its way through the Allegheny Mountains using a series of tunnels, was originally the vision of a railroad man. The tunnel through Laurel Hill was begun with picks and shovels in the 1800s, but the work stopped short when the railroad project fell through. It would be left to the Pennsylvania Turnpike Commission to finish the task fifty-five years later. Eleven men gave their lives to complete the marvel of modern engineering, but it outlived its usefulness after only twenty-four years and was bypassed.

CARS WERE already lined up along the curb of the neat suburban cul-de-sac several houses down the road from Julie and Jim's when Paul and Ian arrived. Ian picked up the paper sack from the back seat as they got out of the car and headed down the road. Carrying a paper sack with a bottle in it was a familiar gesture for Ian. This time, though, it contained sparkling grape juice.

"You know," Ian said, "I think this will be the first new year I'll start without a hangover."

"It's going to be a good year for both of us," Paul said.

Paul had been starting his years since Sara had been gone with a long hangover of his own—a hangover of grief and loneliness. For the first five years, he kept attending Julie's annual party. He painted on a smile, stood to one side, and excused himself at around 12:05. Finally, last year, he had decided not to bother with the act. He had watched the ball drop alone on TV. He didn't want to be social and yet couldn't quite bring himself to go to bed early. He probably should have. It was anticlimactic and depressing. He could hardly believe that one year ago he hadn't even known Ian existed. There was actually a time, not long ago, that Ian had not been a fact of his life.

"Where were you a year ago?" Paul asked.

"You don't really want to know," Ian said.

"Yes, I do."

"No, you don't." They arrived at Julie's door. Ian quickly rang the bell, putting an end to the subject.

Julie was dressed in a long red gown with a dangling rhinestone necklace and matching earrings.

"Hi! Thanks for coming." She took the bottle from Ian and led them to the kitchen to set it down.

"It's grape juice," he said.

"Good for you," she said, looking around behind him. "Where's your date?"

"Paul is my date tonight," he said.

Paul hoped Julie didn't notice his cringe. Would it really be so difficult for Ian to be just a little more careful?

Julie thought nothing of it. "Well, maybe you'll meet someone here tonight," she said. "There are some nice single women. Oh, and here's one now!"

A young girl, about ten or eleven years old, ran up to Julie and hugged her around the legs.

"Megan, do you remember Paul and Ian?"

The girl looked up at Ian. "My mom says I can have some champagne at midnight!"

"That's cool," Ian said. "I'm not allowed, though."

"How come?"

He opened his eyes wide and, with a comical expression, said, "The minister won't let me."

"Megan! Megan!" Megan's little brother, Aiden, ran up to her.

"Go away!" she said.

"Be nice," said Julie.

Aiden looked up at Ian. "You want to see my toys?"

"Yeah, cool!" Ian said.

He went off with the children and sat down on the floor. Paul watched him from across the room as he played with Aiden's toy trucks. Soon there were four other children on the floor with them. Ian made funny faces, and the children laughed.

"Ian! Ian!" Aiden called out to him as he threw a plastic airplane into the air. The kids loved him, and he was great with them.

Before his intellect had a chance to reflect on it, Paul was filled with a powerful longing. He wanted Ian to be the mother of his children. When his brain caught up with his emotions and reminded him of the biological impossibility, he felt a nagging sense of loss.

That Ian would not have children—that the genetic code for his beauty would die with him—seemed like another of God's cruel jokes. It occurred to Paul that beauty called out to our creative instincts. In a desperate fight against life's inevitable decay, beauty demands that we make a copy. Lovers long for children with their beloved. The beautiful inspire artists to write poetry, to compose music, or to paint. Yet even the most moving symphony, the most inspired sculpture, the most elevating theatrical performance does not keep its original alive.

Within each encounter with beauty is the inevitability of loss. The beautiful bouquet of flowers turns brown in a day, the beautiful lover grows old and dies, even the sublime landscape of a mountain is constantly eroded. It will one day return to the flat earth and be nothing.

Paul thought about all the new years that had begun with such hope and promise, the beauty of infinite possibility, that were now distant, set in stone, ancient history. Each year's end was a beginning and each beginning was an end.

"That's a nice necklace," Julie said.

Paul's focus came back to his part of the room. He picked up the gold cross and held it away from this chest to look at it.

"Oh yeah," he said. "It was a Christmas gift."

"I know," Julie said. "I was with Ian when he bought it. Do you like it?"

"Yeah."

"That's good. It seemed like kind of an odd gift."

"Why?"

"I don't know," she said. "I just didn't think men usually bought jewelry for each other."

Paul was trying to decide how to answer when he was saved by the ringing door bell.

"Excuse me," Julie said.

Paul stood near the hors d'oeuvre table, masking his social awkwardness with snacks. He would have liked to have had a glass of wine, but as long as Ian wasn't drinking, Paul wasn't going to either. Ian played with the kids for another hour. Then he got up off the floor and joined Paul near the food.

"You all right?" Ian asked.

"Good," Paul said. "Are you having fun?"

"Yeah," he said. "The kids are great."

"You're good with them."

"They're easy to please. You just pay attention to them and they like you."

"It's almost time!" someone shouted, and everyone headed into the living room to stare at the TV. Paul picked up two glasses and the bottle of sparkling grape juice.

The urgency of the move to the living room amused Paul. New Year's was a one-second holiday. If you weren't glued to the TV at the precise moment, you missed it. It seemed like a complete misunderstanding of the true nature of time.

The countdown had begun: "Ten, nine, eight, seven, six, five, four, three, two, one! Happy New Year!"

The room was filled with the sound of noisemakers and popping corks. Paul opened the sparkling grape juice. Ian held out his glass, and Paul filled it.

"Auld Lang Syne" played through the TV speakers, and all around couples began to embrace. Julie was kissing her husband, Jim. On the other side of the room, Emily kissed her boyfriend, Bob. Marlee was sitting on the couch kissing… who was that guy?

Paul looked at Ian. They shared a knowing smile. Paul raised his glass. "Happy New Year," he said softly.

"Happy New Year."

TATTOO

"And it shall come to pass in that day, that the great trumpet shall be blown, and they shall come which were ready to perish in the land of Assyria, and the outcasts in the land of Egypt, and shall worship the Lord in the holy mount at Jerusalem."

—Isaiah 27:13

ONE AFTERNOON in March, Paul walked into the church commons and found Ian there eating a candy bar and reading the Bible.

"Sorry," he said. "I was just taking a break."

"It's fine with me," Paul said. "Just don't let Julie catch you."

He glanced over his shoulder. No one was behind him, so he stole a quick chocolate-flavored kiss. Then he tapped a finger on the open Bible in front of Ian. He whispered, "Try First Samuel."

He saw Ian in his peripheral vision flipping through the pages as he turned to walk out of the room. He waited just outside the door with his ear tilted in Ian's direction.

"Wow," he heard Ian say. He smiled and went back to his office.

"AND IT came to pass, when he had made an end of speaking unto Saul, that the soul of Jonathan was knit with the soul of David, and Jonathan loved him as his own soul. And Saul took him that day, and would let him go no more home to his father's house. Then Jonathan and David made a covenant, because he loved him as his own soul. And Jonathan stripped himself of the robe that was upon him, and gave it to David, and his garments, even to his sword, and to his bow, and to his girdle."

—1 Samuel 18:1-4

THAT SPRING, Ian enrolled in Paul's Wednesday evening Bible-study class. After dinner, Paul and Ian would ride back to the church. Paul was behind the wheel, of course. Ian sat in the passenger seat clutching his Bible. Their discussion of the evening's passage began before they even got out of the car.

In the class itself, Ian hung on Paul's every word. He asked lots of questions, sometimes so many that no one else had a chance to speak. He kept right on discussing the topic on the ride home, and then in the house, until Paul finally looked at him and said, "Ian, I'm off the clock."

A couple of weeks after the class began, Ian mentioned in passing that Julie was going to take him to the store after work and she would drive him home. Paul thought nothing of it until that evening when they were getting ready for bed. When Ian took off his shirt, Paul noticed that his left shoulder was covered with a gauze bandage.

"What happened to your arm?"

"Nothing." He turned away, trying to hide what Paul had already seen. "I can't show you yet."

"Show me what?"

"It's a surprise."

"But why do you have a bandage on your…. You didn't get a tattoo."

Ian grinned like the cat who swallowed the canary. "You'll like it, I think."

"Why didn't you tell me before?"

"I told you, I wanted to surprise you."

"You got it for me?"

"Yeah, what do you think?"

"I don't know what to say." Paul didn't know what to say because he was fairly sure that when someone tells you he just permanently altered his body as a token of his love for you, the answer he is hoping to hear is not "Why the hell did you do that?"

"It's not my name or anything like that?" Paul asked.

Ian picked at the tape surrounding the gauze. "I'll show you, but it's not very pretty right now." He peeled back the gauze with a slight wince and revealed a heart about three inches across. In its center was a cross.

"You see, it has a double meaning," Ian said. "It's about letting God back into my heart. And you did that. So this is, like, the minister in my heart too."

Paul reached out toward the image. "Don't touch it," Ian said.

"Does it hurt?"

"Yeah, but only for a few days." He taped the gauze back in place. "Do you like it?"

"I really do," Paul said. He really did.

Paul stood outside his own skin, marveling at his life. If anyone had told him a year before that he would be in his bedroom with a twenty-four-year-old guy who had just gotten a tattoo in his honor, he would have told them they were insane. It seemed incomprehensible on so many levels. First of all, Paul hated tattoos....

He could never have imagined that he would be moved almost to tears by such a gesture. What a leap of faith, to put something on your skin that will last forever, certain you'll still want it there in twenty years. No one had ever made such a bold move for him. Paul was afraid he might not live up to it.

When his arm had fully healed, Ian asked Paul to take him to the mall so he could get a shirt without sleeves to show off the new artwork on his shoulder. Ian was immediately drawn to a shop Paul would normally have passed by without even seeing. Its sign was painted in a graffiti style, and the rock music blared a bit too loudly—a tool that was universally employed to drive middle-aged men like him away. Out of all the tank tops in the store, Ian honed in on one with a print of a skull with a knife jammed into the top. Paul shook his head.

"You don't like it?" Ian asked. "I think it's cool."

"Get one with a plain color," Paul was saying as the store clerk walked up. The clerk had bleached white hair, a nose ring, and his right earlobe was stretched by a wide rubber spacer. He had poured himself into bleach-spotted jeans and a camouflage T-shirt, both of which seemed to be two sizes too small. He was clearly gay. "Swishy" was the word that popped into Paul's mind.

I am not like him, Paul thought. He was not sure where the thought came from.

"Hey, Ian," he said. "I haven't seen you in ages. Where have you been?"

Ian knew this guy?

"Oh yeah," Ian said. "I haven't been to the clubs in a while. I'm not drinking anymore."

"No shit?! Ian Fucking Finnerty? Wow. That's great. Since when?"

"Sober six months, almost seven now, right?" Ian asked Paul.

"Right," Paul said.

"Congratulations. That's great. Seriously," the clerk said. "So is this your new boyfriend?"

"Yeah," Ian said, grinning with pride. "This is Paul. Paul—Andy; Andy—Paul."

Boyfriend. Paul immediately hated the word. *Heaven help me*, he thought. *I have a boyfriend.* This clearly should not have come as a surprise. He had been living with Ian for months now. Yet for the most part, they had existed in their own little world. Paul hadn't let himself take much time to consider who they were to the larger world, who each was individually in society, and who they were together. *Ian is my boyfriend.* Paul tried the label on and tried to make himself comfortable with it. It wasn't working.

"Nice to meet you, Paul," Andy said. To Ian, he said, "He's cute."

Andy was part of Ian's other world, a strange foreign place he inhabited that had never included Paul. Andy was ready to accept Paul into their world without hesitation. Paul was sure he didn't belong. *I'm not like him.*

Ian chose three identical tank tops in different colors, and Andy directed them to the fitting room. Ian gestured for Paul to come in with him, which he did.

"Have fun, guys," Andy said and left them alone together.

"Why did you tell him I'm your boyfriend?" Paul asked.

"You are, aren't you?" Ian reached over his shoulders and pulled his T-shirt off over his head.

"Yeah, but you can't go around telling people that."

Ian tried the black tank on first. He was looking at himself from all angles. "Andy doesn't care," he said. "Anyway, who is he going to tell? I doubt you have any mutual friends."

"You never know. We have at least one."

"He won't say anything." He turned so his shoulder faced the mirror to examine the effect of the shirt and the tattoo. He eyed himself critically. "What do you think?"

He was suffering from the delusion that he might not look good in something.

"You look great," Paul said.

"I'm going to try on the brown one," he said, pulling the tank off.

"Why do you need to try it on? They're all the same. They're just different colors."

"I want to see what the color looks like on me."

"It'll look great."

"How do you know?"

"You always look great."

"You're biased."

"Maybe, but I'm not wrong."

As Ian tried on the brown and then the green tank, Paul drifted to his own thoughts. If Paul had a "boyfriend," what was he? Was he gay, straight, bisexual? None of the check boxes seemed quite right. He understood the comic absurdity of his thought: *I'm not gay, but my boyfriend is.* Yet that was how he felt about things. He certainly couldn't insist he was "straight" anymore, given the circumstances. "Bisexual" was the obvious (and least absurd) choice, but it didn't feel right to him either. Paul had always associated that word with people who wanted to play around and experiment with sex. To his mind, it lacked commitment and serious intent.

His sexuality wasn't confusing or complicated at all, really. He had fallen in love with Sara, and he fell in love with Ian. Simple. It only became complicated when he tried to fit that reality into the shorthand of official categories. That these labels failed to describe how he felt about himself should not have troubled him much, but so many people had faith in the categories that he was inclined to believe the problem was with himself and not the check boxes. That was where he became confused.

Ian ended up taking all three shirts. He found the brown tank top most flattering and decided to wear it out of the store. He ripped off the tag and took it up to Andy to ring up.

"You got another tattoo," Andy said. "Nice work."

"Thanks," Ian said. He turned his shoulder toward Andy and gazed over it like an actress posing on the red carpet. He couldn't make such a gesture seriously, so he raised his eyebrows and stuck out his tongue. Andy laughed and blushed.

Paul handed his credit card to the clerk. Something was bothering him, but he couldn't quite put his finger on it. As they walked out of the store, Ian turned his shoulder toward Paul and batted his eyes. "Well, how do I look?"

Paul was distracted. It was something Andy had said. Something had given him the idea that…. Finally, it dawned on him: "He said you got another tattoo."

"What?"

"Andy, he said 'you got another tattoo.'"

"Yeah."

"*Another* tattoo."

Ian looked confused.

"How did he know about the first one?" Paul asked.

"Ah," Ian said.

"I mean, it's—" He gestured toward Ian's hip bone.

"Yeah," he said, putting his hand over the spot. "I don't know. I guess he saw it once."

"How?"

"I don't know."

"You don't know?"

"I don't know."

"Did you sleep with that guy?" Paul was horrified by the idea. *That* guy? Swishy, nose-pierced Andy the shop clerk?

"Can we change the subject?"

"No. Did you?"

"No." Ian's face wrinkled as though he were smelling Limburger cheese. There was more to the story.

"But?"

"Nothing."

"It's not nothing. It's something."

"There was… there was just this one night," Ian said. "It involved a lot of tequila shots. I ended up at his place, but in between the shots and waking up at his place, it's a little fuzzy. He always kind of had a thing for me. I don't know. I don't think anything happened. But that's gotta be, you know, when he saw it. Okay?"

"You don't *think* anything happened, but you don't know. Something might have happened?"

"Some people are kind of prone to blackouts when they drink a lot. I guess I'm one of them."

"So you'd just black out whole nights?"

"Sometimes. Yeah. Later on it got worse. But usually just bits and pieces, details. That night, it's got gaps."

"Like whether or not you had sex."

"Like that. Yeah."

"That's kind of a big gap, isn't it?"

Ian shrugged. His discomfort about the situation made Paul feel better. He believed something must have happened between the two of them that night. Why else would Andy have seen the tattoo? He could handle the idea as long as Ian regretted it. Imagining Ian as a willing participant was hard for Paul to bear. Ian the victim was sympathetic, a fallen angel in need of rescue.

"What's that like," Paul asked, "not knowing?"

"It's weird…. Can we… can we please change the subject now?"

"Yeah. Sorry. Do you want to get lunch at the food court?"

"Yeah."

"You look good in the shirt."

"Thanks."

When they got to the crowded food court, Paul went to stand in line and get their order while Ian looked for a table. This left Paul alone with his thoughts. Falling for Ian, he had inadvertently connected himself to a world he found distasteful and sordid. He imagined the gay clubs with go-go boys, drag queens, backroom sex, and horny men who would take advantage of an angel like Ian because he was drunk and prone to alcoholic blackouts. But did they take advantage? Or had Ian never really tried to say no? Paul felt sick to his stomach. It was as far from Paul's image of himself as his mind could possibly go. If people were to find out about the two of them, would they assume that was his world too?

Not compatible with Christian teaching.

He took the lunch tray and scanned the crowd. He spotted Ian chatting to a group of people at an occupied table. Even from the back, he recognized Julie and her husband, Jim. Ian was gesturing to the new tattoo on his shoulder.

"Hi, Paul!" Julie said as he approached. "You two came together? You must be joined at the hip."

Ian smiled and laughed.

"We're not joined at the hip," Paul snapped. "He just needed a ride because he doesn't have a car."

Julie's mouth fell open. Ian looked away.

Paul could not sleep that night. He sat at his desk reviewing the events of the day. Ian hadn't said anything about Paul's outburst with Julie. He didn't have to. Paul kept playing it over in his head: his overreaction, Julie's surprise, and Ian's disappointment. Julie still did not suspect. She hadn't meant a thing by her comment. It was Paul's own reaction that raised suspicion. If anything was going to give them away, it would be Paul himself.

Paul envied Ian for his openness. The irony was that Ian was probably a better Christian than Paul. He didn't judge. What judgments had Paul made about the clerk, Andy, based on his bleached white hair and feminine mannerisms?

After everything Ian had been through with his mother, he had come out of it unapologetic about who he was. He could stand in a store in the mall and say "This is my boyfriend" without a second thought. Paul wished he could. He tried to imagine what would happen if he stood up in church and said, "This is the new love of my life, Ian Finnerty."

It *was* different for him. This wasn't a clerk in the mall. This was his community, a community that had nourished him most of his adult life. He performed the weddings, the baptisms, the funerals, all the ceremonies that marked the group's support and acknowledgment of the passages of life. Paul had been drawn to the ministry to be part of those rituals, to make sacred the truly meaningful side of life, the part our life of work and business so often fails to value or even acknowledge. The community could make a person feel protected and whole and part of something larger than his own concerns. It was a vehicle for compassion and service. A community can do more than any individual.

Yet many of the same people who stood beside him to bless his union with Sara would shun him if they even suspected his relationship with Ian. The ones who praised him for "helping a troubled kid" would turn their backs if they thought he loved him. It was official church policy not to allow an "avowed, practicing homosexual" to act as minister. He simply couldn't be both a minister and Ian's "avowed" love.

That was the darker side of community. For a group to have a sense of cohesion, a sense of being "us," it has to define what was outside of the group. It has to define a "them"—the excluded. Who "they" are changes over time and from society to society, but the process never changes. It is part of the nature of community life. To have an inside, a tribe must have an outer boundary. For most of the members of Paul's community, young men dancing in gay clubs, people like Andy, were not "us" but "them." Judging by his own reactions, Paul had to admit with some shame that he felt the same way. *I am not like him.*

Paul thought about Jesus, how he ministered to the outcasts, the people on the fringes of society—the poor, the unclean, the prostitutes, and the lepers. Paul had told these stories over and over, but he had never felt the full impact of them until now. How brave and extraordinary an act that was. Jesus didn't have to associate himself with the outcasts. He could have lived a comfortable life as a carpenter, accepted by everyone in his community. He wasn't a beggar or a prostitute or a leper. Yet he chose to associate with them without fear.

If Paul had gained any sympathy for the outsiders, and if he risked being associated with them, it was out of personal interest. He was motivated by his own needs and desires. Jesus included everyone because they needed him, not because he needed them. He risked everything for it. He was willing to give his life. That was love.

How small a sacrifice was being asked of Paul compared to that. Yet for the one person he loved most in the world, Paul could not risk being associated with the outsiders. Where was his courage?

THE

Where does a mountain end? Mountains draw our focus to their snowcapped peaks and present us with the illusion that they are isolated, individual objects. We send postcards and take pictures and try to put a frame around them. But whatever border we create for the natural object we find beautiful is our own projection. The mountain spills out in all directions. It dips into the valley, which rises to the next peak. There is no place where you can stop and say, "The mountain ends here."

PAUL WAS staring at his computer screen. A Word document was open. It contained only one word: "The."

That was as far as Paul had gotten on his sermon before his mind drifted and he forgot what the rest of the opening sentence had been. "The" was clearly not enough to go on.

Church attendance was up. There were many new members—younger members, families with kids. Pledges were up, and the board had decided they just might have enough in the budget to reopen the question of repairing the steeple. There was an open meeting to discuss and vote on the issue planned after services on Sunday.

It seemed like a foregone conclusion now that the steeple repair would be approved, something that had seemed well-nigh impossible only a few months before—before Ian, before Paul's new source of inspiration. He wanted to give one last sermon before the meeting to push things in the right direction.

The.

He must have had some second word in mind when he wrote it. Paul hadn't been stuck on a sermon in quite a while, but his focus on architecture, history, and aesthetics was all too academic, and his mind kept wandering.

He was still thinking about his trip to the mall with Ian, and outsiders like Andy, who had carved out a place for themselves beyond the borders of "respectable" society. He was also thinking about the fearless love Ian had shown when he got that tattoo. He thought about the double meaning, the symbolism. Ian had Christ in his heart (and his heart on his sleeve). There was fearless love in that too. In the middle of this church, trying so hard to be respectable, he wouldn't let anyone rob him of his soul. How many Ians were out there in the world?

Paul began to write. The sermon came to him in a torrent, as though he was taking dictation. That Sunday he stood before the congregation in his black robe and said:

"This afternoon we will be voting on whether or not to approve a budget to repair the old steeple. Fixing that old thing will cost a lot of money. And there are those who will say it is money that could be better spent on something more tangible and practical than beauty. It's a reasonable argument.

"How do you measure the value of beauty? What is it? What does it do? What is it worth? Maybe nothing.

"Or maybe, just maybe, beauty pleases the senses because it reminds us of a divine order and holds a mirror to the face of God."

Paul looked into Ian's eyes as he delivered this line.

"Fixing the steeple will not change the nature of our services, or my sermons, or our community outreach. We don't even see it while we're sitting here in the sanctuary. And that is really the key. Our steeple is not really for us. It is a gift of beauty that we give to the larger community. It is not only for our members or for the people who come through the doors, but for the people who never will.

"A steeple points the way to Heaven. It is a universal symbol that reminds everyone who passes that there is a spiritual dimension to life—that there is something greater than ourselves, and it ties us together across time and across generations.

"To the people who are afraid, who have been alienated from God, who have somehow learned the lesson that Christians are a different kind of people and that Christianity is not for them—let our steeple be a beacon. Let it send them a message.

"Our message is not 'come to our church.' Our message is this: No one lives without a soul. Everyone deserves to feel God's love. No matter who you are, no matter what you do, if you think you have made mistakes, if your wife kicked you out, if you're sick, if you're troubled, if you're black or white, rich or poor—"

The original draft said "straight or gay" here, but Paul lacked the courage to say it and struck it out.

"—God loves you. You are valuable. Your life has meaning. God created you because He needs you.

"That is our message. That is our gift. Our steeple is a gift of beauty to the larger community."

The speech had the desired effect. The members of the congregation voted almost unanimously (Mike Davis was still against it) to fix the steeple. They formed a fund-raising committee then and there and approved taking money from the existing budget to get started on the project as soon as possible.

That evening Paul took Ian to a fancy restaurant to celebrate the victory. Then they came home and made love. Afterward, Paul said, "You know, you inspired that sermon. You and your tattoo."

Ian got up and sat astride Paul. Paul ran his hand over the image on Ian's arm.

"So I'll be getting that trip to Tahiti soon?" Ian asked.

"We'll see," Paul said, brushing Ian's hair back behind his shoulders.

"We could go to Provincetown, Massachusetts. We can get married there."

"Why not Iowa?"

"The ocean is sexier than corn."

Paul's face became serious. "Do you want to get married?"

"Do you?" His eyes were wide with expectation.

Paul's heart sank. As he searched for just the right words, his face gave him away.

"I was just joking around," Ian said. He rolled off of Paul and lay down beside him, looking up at the ceiling.

Paul turned to him, resting his head on his elbow. "I would if I could."

"I understand. There's Sara, the love of your life, and then there's whatever I am. The troubled kid you're helping out."

"That's not fair."

"You're right. It's not."

Paul sighed deeply. How had that happened? How had the mood shifted so quickly? He was trying to decide whether to argue this one out or to leave it there and turn off the light. They weren't going to resolve this in one night, and things would be back to normal in the morning. The only difference would be how much sleep they got.

Ian made the decision for him. "I'm tired," he said. "Why don't we just go to sleep?"

"You know I love you," Paul said.

"I know," Ian said, and he reached over and switched off the light.

Ian drifted off into gentle snoring, but Paul lay awake. He was thinking about his wedding to Sara. How beautiful she had been in her mother's wedding gown, with the cascade of tiny white baby's breath in her hair. He remembered the little flower girls and ring bearer who had added an element of chaos to the event by stopping midway down the aisle and deciding, right at that moment, to lie down on the floor. During the months that Sara had been frantically planning the pageant of the wedding, Paul had wondered if they wouldn't be better off eloping and getting it over with. He had not been prepared for how powerful it would be on the day to be surrounded by all the people who loved him and to have his entire community welcoming them into their lives as a married couple.

This new love was every bit as powerful as the love he had felt for Sara. Yet he was trying to contain it, to keep it in a bubble, separate from the rest of his life. The result was dozens of tiny rejections. "This is Ian, a young man I've been helping out." That was the worst one of all. It not only distanced Ian, it minimized him. Paul was afraid Ian might start to have doubts about their relationship, but he didn't know how to stop the rejections.

CHUCK THE MAILMAN

What is religion but the form? What is it but the mountain? Paul was attracted to the church as Edmund Hillary was to Everest. Being a church member was not enough. He had to climb to the top because it was there. He had to be a minister. Learning the rituals, the sacred texts, the history: they're not the essence of faith but tools—like a mountaineer's pickax and rope—that help you inch along the surface. Paul had never realized what it would mean to have people looking up to him. Fall, and what a long way down it is. At least at the top of the mountain, people are aware of the danger. Any mountain climber will tell you that the summit is only the halfway point. You still need to make it down safely. But with religion, when you get to the top, no one expects you to stumble. No one told Paul he was only halfway there.

PERSONAL CARS, UPS trucks, and delivery vans were always driving in and out of the church parking lot, but the mail truck had its own distinctive sound. The mail was never earth-shattering, but as soon as he heard the postal engine, Paul felt compelled to immediately leap up and walk out to Julie's desk to collect it. It was a landmark in his day. Julie had a good rapport with Chuck, the regular postal carrier. He was blond, slim, probably around thirty, with feminine mannerisms. He and Julie would usually chat for a few minutes before he continued on his route. Paul had always been too focused on the mail to pay much attention to the person who delivered it.

On this day, mailman and minister happened to converge on the office as Ian walked past the window, pushing the lawn mower. It was hot outside, and Ian had taken off his shirt and had it hanging off his hip through a belt loop. He peered into the office window and waved as he went by.

"Ooh, he has his shirt off!" Julie said.

Emily giggled. "He is so cute!"

Chuck handed the bundle of letters and magazines to Julie, who separated the third from the first-class mail in one motion and gave the letters to Paul.

"Hi, Chuck!" she said to the mailman with a genuine smile.

Chuck leaned on the reception desk. "How are you doing today?"

"Great," Julie said, gesturing in the direction of the window. "We're watching our custodian cut the lawn. That's how we pass our day around here."

"He's fun to watch," Emily chimed in.

Chuck gazed out the window and watched as Ian made another pass with the mower. He chuckled.

"Well, don't get too excited, girls," he said, adding in a stage whisper, "he bats for the other team."

"Really? Are you sure?" Julie asked.

"From personal experience," Chuck said, raising his eyebrows.

Paul took a deep breath. He wanted to punch the satisfied smirk off the mailman's face. In fact, he wasn't that kindly disposed to the entire postal service at the moment. To avoid glaring at the mailman, he glared at the mail in his hand. He hoped this might pass for intense concentration on his personal correspondence. He should have gone back into his office right then, but he couldn't bring himself to leave—he didn't want to hear another word and he didn't want to miss a thing. Both Emily and Julie were now focused completely on Chuck, their eyes wide.

"You mean…," Emily said.

"He's pretty," Chuck said, more to himself than to Emily or Julie, "but he's kind of a train wreck."

Paul bit the inside of his cheek. A train wreck? How dare he? Paul comforted himself with a daydream of stabbing the mailman through the neck with a letter opener.

"He's not now," Julie said. "He's not drinking now. I think he's really turned things around. He's really nice."

"That's good," Chuck said, still gazing out the window. "I hope he has. Well, neither rain nor sleet nor dark of night, or whatever it is." Then he gave a little wave and continued on his route.

"Wow." Julie turned to Paul, delighted with this bit of juicy gossip. "Did you know he was gay?"

"No," he said, and he retreated into his office still holding everybody's mail. He could hear the muffled voices and giggles of the two women through the closed door. He couldn't make out what they were saying, but the pitch and tone suggested the topic had not changed. He slumped into his chair and rested his forehead on his palms. His emotions came at him in a confusing jumble. Why had he lied? Why didn't he say of course he'd known Ian was gay, like it was no big deal? He felt guilty. He was afraid. The gossip had started. How long could it be before it involved him too? They would be giggling behind his back soon, and that would only be the beginning.

The expression "train wreck" played over and over in his head. A train wreck? What was the mailman alluding to? How well did he know Ian? Had Chuck been burned in a terrible romance, or had it been a one-night stand? Neither option made him feel any better.

Paul couldn't get any work done for the rest of the day. He was too busy torturing himself with thoughts of late-night drunken arguments that hinted at emotional intimacy and ridiculous images of Ian stripping off Chuck's postal uniform and performing all manner of sexual acts on him. It made his stomach turn, but he could not keep himself from picking at the mental wound.

At the end of the day, Ian got into Paul's car for the ride home with a big smile as though nothing had happened. After all, nothing had. Ian tried to chat, but Paul could not focus on anything he had to say.

"What's wrong?" Ian finally asked.

"Nothing."

"Something's wrong."

"Don't worry about it."

"Is it about me?"

"I told you, it's nothing."

For about a mile, Paul didn't speak. Ian glanced at him, then at his feet, then back at Paul. Finally he could take no more. "What? What did I do?"

Paul shook his head. He knew better, but he couldn't restrain himself. "Tell me about Chuck."

"Chuck who?"

"Chuck the mailman."

"Chuck the mailman? What are you talking about?"

"He delivers the mail to the church. You haven't seen him there?"

"No."

"You don't know him?"

"I don't get it. Do you think I'm cheating on you or something?"

"He says he knows you."

"How?"

"Very well, apparently."

"I don't know anybody named Chuck. What, this just happened to come up while he was delivering the mail?"

"As a matter of fact...."

"That's crazy."

"He saw you mowing the lawn. He said he knew you before. He *knew* you before. Is it true?"

"You're telling me the guy who delivers the mail came in and mentioned in passing that he fucked me?"

"Yeah."

"To the minister? He just walked in and said *to the minister*, 'Here's the mail, and by the way, I fucked your custodian'?"

"Not like that, but basically, yeah."

"I don't believe you."

"You're avoiding my question."

"I don't know. I don't remember. Maybe."

"How can you not know?"

"That's a stupid question," Ian said, crossing his arms across his chest. "I'm sorry, it just is."

"How could you just...."

"Just what? Have a life before I met you? What do you want me to do about it? You're talking about the past. What exactly do you want me to do about it now? Do you have a time machine?"

"No."

"Well then, shut up."

Ian tightened his jaw and turned to face the window. They rode the rest of the way home in silence. When they got back into the house, Ian went immediately into the kitchen and started preparing dinner, banging the bowls and pans as he went. Paul sat in the living room for a while, listening to the slamming drawers and the vigorous chopping. When the noise had died down sufficiently, Paul went into the kitchen. Ian was standing at the stove with his back to the door, browning hamburger and chopped onions in a frying pan. He didn't turn around.

Paul leaned against the door frame. "I'm sorry," he said.

Ian kept right on pushing the food around with the spatula.

"Look at me," Paul said.

Ian turned. There were tears on his cheeks.

"You're crying," Paul said.

"It's the onions," Ian said, wiping his cheek with the back of his hand. He turned back to the hamburger.

Paul approached him from behind, swept his long hair back, and kissed the side of his neck.

Ian snapped his shoulder back and moved away.

"I'm sorry," Paul said. "It's my fault. I was jealous."

Ian finally turned to speak to him. His eyes were red and puffy, his brow pinched. "You were supposed to be the one person who doesn't hold my past against me. Everyone else can think…. I don't even know what they think of me. But you. I thought it was different with you. I thought you saw me… that I could be a new person with you. But I can't. It's all still there just waiting to come back at me."

Now Paul's eyes welled up. "I never want to make you feel that way."

"Yeah, well, you did," Ian said, turning again to his skillet.

"Hey," Paul said. He reached across Ian and turned off the gas, then picked up the skillet and moved it to the cold back burner. He took Ian by the shoulders. "You don't understand at all. Listen to me. Are you listening? I remember when you first walked into my church, the very first time. For a minute, I actually thought you were an angel. Even when you were drinking, I couldn't stop thinking about you. I never thought this could happen. I don't think badly of you. Are you crazy? I love you. It was love at first sight. That's why I get so jealous. It hurts me to think about the other men."

"Well then, don't," Ian said. "I don't. I'm with you. I'm only with you."

BLOOD DRIVE

"And the second angel sounded, and as it were a great mountain burning with fire was cast into the sea: and the third part of the sea became blood."

—Revelation 8:8

RELLA PETERS vibrated. She was a thin woman in her midsixties. Thin, no doubt, because her nervous energy burned every calorie off before it had a chance to settle. Her synapses were constantly firing, taking her from one thought to the next without…. She would start talking about the chairs in the sanctuary and then…. You know, she has a son in Florida who makes benches and…. The service was very nice, but that song the choir sang reminded her of…. Oh, when were they going to be having the fall rummage sale this year? Because she needed to…. You know, she meant to sign up for the donations to the homeless shelter but…. Did that coffee order ever come in?

Being a minister meant dealing with all kinds of personalities. Paul managed to find a method to interact with almost everyone: the depressed ones, the brusque ones, the falsely cheery ones. Then there was the category he privately labeled "extra grace" people. He needed to summon extra grace from God to deal with them. The one personality type he found hardest to cope with was nervousness. The vibes nervous people gave off put him so on edge that he wanted to go screaming and running the other way. Rella combined her vibrating with the even more annoying habit of standing about one inch too close. She would start talking to a person at one end of the social hall. They would back off an inch; she would move forward. They would back up again, and by the end of the conversation, she had her poor companion pinned to the far wall, unable to retreat any farther.

Rella poured her energy into just about every committee in the church. Paul could not escape her. When he knew he was going to have to meet her, he would plan ahead by taking deep breaths and centering himself with the mantra "She is a good soul. She is a good soul."

Sometimes, though, she approached him on a Sunday, when Paul had had no time to prepare.

"Paul! Paul!"

"Jesus, help me," Paul muttered.

"About the Worship Committee meeting, I was thinking about the music that if we…. Did you see the order form for new hymnals, I think we ought to…. I'm so glad we decided to fix the steeple, by the way…. Your sermon about that was so…. Do you have a transcript of it, I'd like to…. Do you think they need a treasurer for the Fund-raising Committee because…. I did that for the Rummage Committee, you know, and…."

Paul was standing with his eyes wide, backing up half inch by half inch, glancing over his shoulders for an escape route.

"Excuse me, Rella." Thank God for Ian. "I'm sorry to interrupt. But Emily needed to talk to Paul for a minute."

"I owe you one," Paul whispered as they walked over to the table where Emily was seated. She and Margaret Fletcher, one of the church's most generous donors, were manning the table to sign people up for the annual blood drive.

"Ian, are you going to sign up for the blood drive?" Emily asked.

"Oh, I would but I can't," he said.

"Why not?"

"They don't let you if you're gay," he said.

Although the rumor mill had done its work and everyone in the church now knew about Ian's sexuality, it was the first time anyone had heard him directly acknowledge it himself. Emily blushed. Margaret glanced around uncomfortably. Paul turned pale. He was looking at the sign-up sheet and the time slot where he had written his own name— the very first slot of the day. Ian followed his gaze. When Paul glanced up, their eyes locked.

"If you've had sex with another man, you're not allowed," he said directly to Paul. Both women giggled nervously at the mention of sex with men.

"I didn't realize that," Paul said softly.

"Sorry," Ian said. He wasn't apologizing that he couldn't give. He was apologizing for changing Paul's life. He walked off, back to the supply closet.

Until she got sick, Sara had been the driving force behind the annual blood drives. Paul and Sara used to kick off every blood drive as the first donors, leading by example. After her death, Paul had continued the tradition himself. Encouraging community service and giving was one of the most meaningful parts of his job. It was a ritual the church counted on him to provide. Having to sit the blood drive out filled him with a profound sense of loss. And it made him feel dirty, like a person from biblical times who'd been labeled unclean.

His thoughts were interrupted by the two women at the table in front of him.

"I can't believe he said that in church," Margaret said, shaking her head.

"Didn't you know he was gay?" Emily asked.

"I'd heard something about it. I just don't see why people have to talk about it like that," Margaret said. "I don't care what people do, but why do they have to talk about it all the time? It used to be that people just kept it to themselves. I mean, I'm heterosexual. You don't see me going around advertising who I have sex with." She looked at Paul, expecting his agreement.

"That's a nice wedding ring you have," he said. "Excuse me."

He left the crowded lobby, crossed the courtyard with his eyes on the ground, hoping no one would greet him, and found a quiet spot in an empty classroom. He sat looking at the posters of shepherds in pastel robes and Noah's cartoon ark with its smiling giraffes, hippos, and elephants standing two by two. Their whole hippo and giraffe communities were about to be wiped out. Didn't that pair of smiling lions have a doomed pride back home that loved and cared for them? What did they have to smile about? He sat with his head down, letting the emotions wash over him in waves of anger, sadness, shame, and fear. He was the same person he had always been. How could one choice make him seem suddenly different to the world?

Paul heard the door swinging open. He sat up straight, hoping to seem as though he had an official reason for sitting in an empty classroom in a child-sized chair. He slouched back down when he realized it was Ian, pushing a mop and bucket. Ian, not expecting anyone to be in the room, gasped and jumped back. "What are you doing in here? You scared me to death!"

"Hiding."

"I'm mopping."

"I see that. How come you never do that at home?"

"You don't do sermons at home," Ian said.

Paul rolled his eyes.

"Why are you hiding?" asked Ian. "Is it the blood thing?"

"What am I going to do about it?"

"You could lie on the form, I guess," Ian said as he rang out the mop.

"I don't want to do that. That's not right."

"You can say you're anemic or something, or you have the flu."

"But what about next time?"

"A really bad flu. One of those one-year flus. Tell them you suddenly realized you're Haitian." Ian took the mop over to the far side of the room and let it flop down onto the tiles.

"You're not helping."

"Well, why am I making up lies for you? You can come up with your own lies."

"Are you upset that I'm lying?"

"It is what it is, Paul," Ian said as he pushed the mop along. "It is what it is."

Paul watched Ian long enough for the clean mop water to become slate gray. It had a smell reminiscent of, but not entirely analogous to, a locker full of dirty socks. As much as Ian scrubbed, Paul could see no difference, except for the fact that before the tile floor was caked with ground-in dirt and was dry, and now it was caked with ground-in dirt and was wet.

"You're in my way," Ian said, purposely sloshing the mop onto Paul's feet under the table.

"Thanks," he said, lifting his wet shoes up onto one of the tiny chairs across from him. Then he went on as though there had been no pause in their conversation. "Do they really just assume that anyone who is gay has AIDS?"

Ian stopped mopping and leaned, resting his weight on the mop handle. "I don't know. They're just overly cautious, I guess."

"It doesn't bother you?"

"I guess I have more important things to worry about than what the bureaucrats at the Red Cross think of my sex life."

"How often does that happen?"

"What?"

"People… they assume you're different—something's wrong with you?"

"Oh." He paused to think about it. "Not very often, really."

Paul wasn't entirely convinced.

"Seriously," Ian said. "Every once in a while there's something. There was my mom…. But you choose your friends, you know? You okay?"

"It's just new to me."

"Yeah," Ian said. He dragged the mop back to the bucket and let it rest in the dirty-sock water.

"Have you…," Paul started to ask.

"What?"

"I mean, have you… been tested?"

Ian burst out laughing. He placed a palm on his forehead, shook his head, then ran the hand over his face until it stopped over his mouth.

"What are you laughing at?"

"I'm sorry. Sorry. Serious. Yes. I have. At rehab. I'm fine. We're fine."

"What's so funny?"

"It's just, as a rule, I think you're supposed to ask that before you have sex with somebody, not after you've been living together for, like, half a year."

"You didn't ask me."

"You were a virgin."

"I was not a virgin."

"You were a guy virgin. I popped your cherry."

Paul rolled his eyes.

"Come on, say it. 'I lost my virginity to Ian Finnerty.'"

"I'm not going to say that."

"Say it: 'Ian took my virginity.'"

"No."

"'Ian made me a man.'"

"Are you going to shut up if I don't say it?"

"No."

"Fine. Ian Finnerty took my virginity."

"'Ian made me a man.'"

"Ian made me a man."

"Was that so hard?"

Paul smiled and shook his head.

Ian's playful expression changed. "Are you… sorry I did?"

"How could you ask that? No. Not in a million years."

"He loves me," Ian sang like a kindergartner.

"You're a goofball."

"But you love me! Enjoy your hiding." Ian pushed the mop bucket out of the room singing "Like a Virgin" (off-key) as he went.

Paul laughed. He felt much better.

CHOPSTICKS AND SUSHI

Mountains are storm gatherers. In the winter, storms bring high winds and deep, blowing snow. In warm weather, afternoon thunderstorms bring flash floods. Hikers on high mountains, usually the tallest objects, are often struck by lightning. The hiker who starts up the mountain on a clear sunny day may find himself suddenly, without warning, in inches or feet of snow. Storms on the mountain come without warning.

AS PAUL filled his plate with rice, egg rolls, and salt-and-pepper shrimp, Ian explored the back of the Great Wall Buffet. The back was where they kept the salad bar and the trays of sushi. He filled his plate with an assortment, plus seaweed salad and miniature octopus from the salad bar. He sat down at the booth armed with two sets of chopsticks in red paper sleeves.

"Here," he said, offering one of the sets of chopsticks to Paul.

"I don't need those," Paul said. He reached out to take the fork and knife, neatly wrapped in a napkin and fastened with a green paper ring, from the table.

Ian snatched it away from him.

"Yes, you do," he said, holding the cutlery up over his right shoulder.

"Give that back."

"No, use these." He put the chopsticks down on the table in front of Paul.

"What is that you're eating?" Paul asked.

"Sushi. What are you eating?"

"Real food." Paul pulled a napkin from a black dispenser on the table and put it on his lap.

"You have no adventure in your soul," Ian said.

"Not for raw fish and octopus, no. Give me my fork."

"No," Ian said. "That's cheating." He tossed the silverware over his shoulder onto the table of the booth next to them. It landed with a clatter and bounced onto the seat. He took his own chopsticks out of the sleeve, picked up a piece of raw salmon bound to a ball of rice with a strand of seaweed, dipped it into the green dot of wasabi sauce on his plate, and popped it into his mouth.

Paul shook his head. He took the chopsticks out of the paper sleeve and looked at them with suspicion.

"You do it like this," Ian said, moving his index finger to manipulate the top of the two chopsticks in his hand. "It's kind of like holding a pencil."

Paul tried to pick up a piece of shrimp and sent it skidding across his plate. Ian reached over and snapped it up with his own chopsticks and popped it in his mouth.

"Hey!"

"You'd better learn fast or I'm going to get all your food."

"I can't do it. Give me my fork back."

Ian put down his chopsticks, reached over, wrapped his own hands around Paul's, and manipulated the chopsticks for him. "Like this," he said. "Only the top one moves. You hold the bottom one still. See? Try it."

Paul made a few practice grasps at his shrimp. He managed to get one in his mouth, although without much finesse. The second shrimp ended up in his lap.

"Where did you learn to do this?" Paul asked, clicking the chopsticks together.

"When I lived in China."

"Really?"

Ian tilted his head and gave the "duh!" expression. "You're cute," he said, then shrugged. "Someone taught me."

"Someone?"

"Yeah."

"A guy?"

"I think he was male."

"Was he your…?"

"Why do you ask me those things if you don't want to know?" Ian grabbed one of the two egg rolls from Paul's plate with his chopsticks. "Ah-ha!"

"Stop that! Eat your dead fish."

Ian grasped a miniature octopus in his chopsticks and pointed it toward Paul. "Try one. They taste kind of like shrimp."

He wrinkled his nose. "No, thank you."

Ian tossed it into his mouth.

"How can you eat that? I hope you don't expect me to kiss you after that."

"I absolutely do," he said as he picked up another octopus. He put this one on the center of his tongue, which he stuck out at Paul.

"You really like that? Or are you just torturing me?"

"Does it have to be one or the other? I like it. Torturing you is a fringe benefit. Have you ever even tried sushi?"

"No."

"How do you know you don't like it?"

"I just do." Paul was now stabbing at a shrimp with one end of a single chopstick.

"There are a lot of things you'd never tried when you met me. You seem to like those a lot now."

"True. True. But I don't think sushi is going to be one of those things."

"Just try one. They're not all raw. Try this one—it's mild." He picked up a piece of white sushi and held it out toward Paul's mouth.

"What is it?"

"Try it first."

"What is it?"

"It's eel."

Paul turned his head. "No, thank you."

Ian popped the eel into his own mouth.

Paul was trying in vain to pick up fried rice with his chopsticks. "C'mon, Ian. I'm hungry. Please give me my fork back."

"What will you give me?"

"What do you want?"

Ian quickly raised and lowered his eyebrows. It was clear from Ian's expression that he wanted Paul to pay his fork ransom that night in bed.

"Yes, fine. Whatever you want. Just give me the fork, sadist!"

Ian did not reach over and get the fork. Instead, he picked up one of the shrimp from Paul's plate with his own chopsticks and fed it to him. Their eyes lingered on each other's as Ian slid the chopsticks slowly from Paul's lips.

"Paul?"

Paul turned. It was Mike Davis. He and his wife, Janice, were standing by the table. How long had they been there?

"Hi," Paul said, sitting up straight. He put his hand over his mouth as if by doing so he could hide the evidence of the moment before.

"I thought that was you," Mike said. He shuffled from one foot to another. It was an unusual stance for someone who was usually so commanding. They had obviously been there long enough.

"Hi, Ian," said Janice. Mike stole a glance at Ian out of the corner of his eye but did not acknowledge him directly.

For a moment, the four diners looked at one another with stupid wide grins, waiting for someone to speak.

"So," Janice said, "do you guys eat here a lot?"

"No," Paul said. "Not really." Another awkward silence.

Mike nodded his head. "Well, we'd better go get our food."

"Yeah," Paul said. "Nice to see you."

The mood now broken, Paul got up and picked up a set of cutlery from a nearby table. When Mike and Janice returned to their booth, Paul watched them out of the corner of his eye. They leaned into each other as though they were speaking in hushed tones. From time to time, they would glance over to Paul and Ian's booth and then quickly look back to their plates.

"Don't look so guilty," Ian said. "We weren't doing anything wrong."

"Do I look guilty?"

"Like you were caught with your hand in the cookie jar."

Paul put his right hand on his cheek, trying to feel the emotion on his skin.

"You have a terrible poker face," Ian said, drawing a circle around Paul's face in the air with his chopsticks. "Everything you think is right there."

The waitress, a young Chinese woman without much English, approached the table. She was holding the bill on a small plastic tray with two fortune cookies on top. Without asking, she set it down in front of Paul. She took their empty plates and went back to the kitchen.

Ian unwrapped one of the fortune cookies and cracked it open. "'Everything has beauty,'" he read, "'but not everyone sees it.'" He shrugged and set the slip of paper down next to the used chopsticks. "What does yours say?"

Paul cracked open his cookie. He read the fortune to himself and chuckled at its appropriateness.

"Well?" Ian asked. "What's it say?"

"'Never regret anything that made you smile.'"

The following Sunday, after the sermon, Paul stood to the side at coffee hour, as he usually did. Socializing after the service had never been his favorite part of the job. Although he felt great compassion for people and was fascinated by their personalities and idiosyncrasies, he was much better in front of an entire group, speaking about life in general, than he was chatting with people one-on-one. He loved the philosophical side of the ministry, studying theology, motivating people collectively with sermons. Sara had been the outgoing one. She had made it possible for him to hide in a corner with a cup of coffee because she took up the social slack. Parishioners would have a short conversation with Paul and a long one with Sara and then remember their positive experience with the minister and his wife as a unit. After she died, Paul's solitary nature was more noticeable.

Paul watched Ian from across the room. He was not like any custodian the church had had. He attended services every Sunday. He greeted the church members and guests as they came through the door. (A couple of grouches in the church wondered if it was appropriate for "the janitor" to greet guests, but almost everyone else enjoyed it.) He knew everyone by name and could remember the names of their kids and grandkids. Ian was hard not to like. As he folded chairs and wiped up coffee spills, everyone he passed smiled and said hello. When he lifted the trash bag out of the bin, two church members stepped over to help.

Paul flashed back to a moment years ago when Sara had stood in the exact same spot, wearing a sleeveless yellow dress with flowers. Paul's favorite. It was a potluck supper. Sara talked to each guest and gave them specific compliments on their dishes. She made a point, of course, to try them all. She asked for recipes and remembered exactly what the people brought the year before, even if they could not remember themselves. Sara was a perfect complement to Paul, both in his life and in his ministry. They were a powerful pair.

Paul returned to the present and saw Ian joking with the third-graders over the little cups of apple juice. Paul felt lucky and proud. Of all the people in the room who cared for Ian in some small fashion, only Paul knew him as well as he did. They had glimpses of Ian's beauty, but only Paul had the full picture.

Ian complemented Paul just as Sara had. He was outgoing and personable. He drew people to him. Paul pictured Ian at a similar potluck, greeting each guest on their collective behalf, remembering their best recipes and the personal stories behind them. He imagined Ian teaching a religious education class, as Sara sometimes had, entertaining the kids with puppets. He pictured Ian shaking hands with the visitors on Christmas Eve and cohosting a holiday dinner at their home for the staff. Ian would remember the names of spouses and cousins and grandkids, and Paul would give the perfect speech thanking them for their work over the course of the year. They would be the perfect team. Ian could be the one to bring Paul closer to his community.

Paul followed Ian with his eyes as he walked to the front of the social hall. As he turned, he noticed Julie in the far corner talking with Mike and Janice Davis. He couldn't hear what they were saying, but as they spoke, they glanced at Ian and then at Paul. There was something about their posture that told Paul that he was the topic of their gossip. He could not pinpoint exactly what gave them away, but even from a distance he knew they were talking about what they had seen the other night at the Chinese buffet. His dream of the church welcoming Ian as his equal partner vanished in the harsh light of day. Paul left the social hall and retreated to his office. He shut the door and sat gazing at the Botticelli portrait tacked to his wall.

Fifteen minutes later, there was a knock on the office door. It was Julie. She stood in the door frame, massaging the joints of her right hand with her left.

"Can I talk to you for a minute?"

Paul didn't remember any good conversations that started that way, but he gave an open smile and waved her in. "Sure, what's on your mind?"

Julie sat down in one of the chairs in front of Paul's desk. She picked up a paperweight and looked at it. She was having trouble making eye contact. "Well, I'm sure no one really takes any of this seriously, but you know people talk."

"About what?"

"Well…." She set the paperweight back on the desk. "You know that everyone knows about Ian… that he's gay."

"Okay."

"Mike was talking about it just now. It's not just Mike. It's obvious you two are close, and so there are rumors… because he's gay."

"Rumors?"

Julie brushed an invisible strand of hair away from her forehead. "He obviously has a crush on you."

"Obviously?"

"You haven't noticed."

"No."

"It's obvious to everyone else."

"It is?"

"Yeah. And it makes sense that he'd feel that way. It's like when people fall in love with their therapists. What is that?"

"Transference?"

"Yeah. That's it. You've helped him a lot."

Paul took a pen out of the pencil holder on his desk and tapped it on the day planner. "What did Mike say exactly?"

"Oh," Julie said, blushing. "He said he ran into you at a restaurant. He said…. He thought…. He said it looked like you were on a date."

"What did you say?"

"I said that I thought he was kind of like a son to you. I mean, that's right, isn't it? But you should be careful, you know?"

"Careful of what?"

"I don't mean that anyone really believes anything is happening between the two of you. But I'm wondering what Ian thinks is going on. I mean, he might be getting attached in a way you're not comfortable with. You don't want to lead him on. It's not fair to him."

"I don't really think that's what's happening. But thanks for letting me know about this." He opened his palm and gestured toward the door.

Julie stood up to go. Before she opened the door, she turned and said, "I wouldn't worry about it. It's just gossip. But I thought you should know."

"I'm not worried," he said.

Paul was worried. He was very worried.

THE DATE

"Many enter the Garden of Love thru the wrong gate.... Imagination often leads us into the wrong path.... Just on the other side of the Valley of Doubt lies the Mountain of Jealousy, which springs forth from lack of faith, understanding, and forgetfulness."
          —*W. D. Gann,* The Tunnel Thru the Air

"I HAD a weird conversation with Julie today," Ian said as he got into Paul's car after work the following Thursday. "She wanted to know if I had a crush on you."

"She asked you that?"

"Yeah."

"What did you tell her?"

"I told her you were the best lover I ever had."

Paul was startled. Ian took one look at his expression and gave him an amused head shake and eye roll. "That was a joke, Paul. I think I need to make signs that say 'joke' so I can hold them up for you."

"What did you tell her?"

"I lied," Ian said. "Just good friends."

"Is that what you said? 'Just good friends'?"

"Something like that. Can we try Thai today? I'm sure they have something you can eat. I'm in the mood for something spicy."

"You know, why don't we just go home and order a pizza."

"I want to go out. We always eat out on Thursday."

"I just think… I'd rather go home."

"Does this have something to do with what I said about Julie? You're upset about it?"

"It just seems like there are a lot of rumors going around right now."

"So?"

"I'd just like to let things die down a little bit. Maybe be a little less visible for a while."

"That's really why? You really don't want to go because people might see us? You're fucking kidding me."

"It's not…. Why don't we just go home and order a pizza and then we can make popcorn and watch a movie. I think it would be nice."

"Sure, that's nice. I like doing that, but not every night. You did all kinds of things with Sara. I've seen the pictures."

"That was different. She was…."

"What?"

"A woman, Ian. She was a woman. Come on, you live in the same world I do."

"I think you're overestimating how interested people are in your life. Most people are too busy with their own lives. You're not that fascinating."

"Julie asked you about it, didn't she?"

"She works with us every day. She's my friend. This is insane. You mean we can't ever go anywhere together? I don't want to just sit in front of the TV every night. I'm not old enough for that yet. I'll feel like a prisoner."

He was pouting like a boy. That tactic had almost always worked in the past, but Paul had started to build up defenses to Ian's face.

"Maybe you should call a friend and go out sometime," Paul said. "You and I are together practically twenty-four hours a day. It might be a good idea for you to spend time with other friends."

It was such a logical and perfect suggestion that Paul made it out of pure momentum. He wanted so much to put an end to the current discussion that he didn't really think things through. The last thing Paul wanted was for Ian to start going out with a bunch of fun, attractive young people. As soon as he said it, he hoped Ian would reject the idea.

"Maybe I will," he said.

When they got home, Ian sat cross-legged on the futon and scrolled through names in his cell phone address book. Paul dug in the drawer for pizza menus, trying not to watch. Ian would scroll down to a name, then look up and furrow his brow in contemplation, then go back to scrolling. His list of numbers seemed fairly long. Whose numbers were they? Paul knew nothing about them. Every number in that phone became an old lover—a younger, more exciting, and sexier lover. Any one of them could take Ian's life in a new direction with the right word or suggestion. That direction might not include Paul. He was beginning to wish he had just gone ahead and taken Ian to the restaurant in the first place.

Finally, Ian stopped scrolling. He squinted at the phone's screen for a moment and chewed on the nail of his index finger. He finally pushed the Send button, flipped his hair back, and put the phone to his ear. He tapped his left fingers on his knee as he waited for an answer.

"Hi, Ray?" he said. "It's Ian." Only "Ian." No last name. "Yeah, I know. How are you?" Then Ian jumped to his feet and went into the bedroom.

Why was he taking the call in another room? Paul told himself it was none of his business what Ian and this Ray were talking about. It was natural to want privacy, wasn't it? It didn't mean anything.

He called and ordered the pizza. When he finished, Ian was still on the phone. He heard laughter coming from the bedroom. They were laughing. What were they laughing about? Paul was consumed with the preposterous notion that the laughter was about him. Would Ian really be laughing about Paul only a few feet away? He drifted to the bedroom door, standing just close enough to hear Ian's half of the conversation and just far enough to maintain plausible deniability if Ian suddenly walked out. He held the pizza menu up to his face and looked in its direction without focus. He was ashamed to be listening, but he could not help himself.

"Really? How is she? ... You're kidding, twins? ... No, I haven't talked to him in ages. ... Are you still in touch with Brad?"

Paul was relieved and disappointed: relieved that he hadn't heard anything incriminating but disappointed because he felt certain that he had simply missed the important part of the conversation—the part where Ian confessed that he was miserable with the old man and that he missed having fun with his friends.

Ian was still chatting when the delivery driver arrived. Paul paid for the pizza, put plates out on the table, sat, and waited. Finally Ian emerged with a big smile on his face.

"I'm going to go out with my friend Ray tomorrow," he said.

"Who is Ray?" Paul asked, hoping it didn't sound like an inquisition.

"We were really good friends a while ago," Ian said.

"What happened?"

"He tried to convince me I had a problem with alcohol. I told him to fuck off and mind his own business. Turns out one of us was right," he said, grabbing two pieces of pizza and letting them flop onto his plate. "I was a little bit scared to call him, but he was actually glad to hear from me."

"Well, that's great. It's good that you're getting together," Paul said.

The following evening Ian paced as he waited for Ray's arrival. Ian looked radiant. He was wearing a shirt Paul had never seen him put on before. It was an Asian floral pattern reminiscent of tattoo art. It had the same intriguing mix of masculine and feminine aspects as Ian's own face. His hair was neatly combed, his eyes were wide, and he was full of youth and energy. Paul felt dowdy and old.

When the bell rang, Ian went to the door. Paul did not follow him. Out of the corner of his eye, he could see Ian greet the guest with a hug. A hug!

Ian led his friend into the living room. "This is Paul," he said.

Ray was a nightmare. He was about Ian's age, with dark curly hair and big brown eyes. He was of some vague ethnicity that Paul couldn't quite place. Maybe half Indian or Hispanic or perhaps Middle Eastern. His beige skin was flawless. He was almost comically handsome. He might even have been better-looking than Ian, if such a thing were possible. Together they looked as though they were headed off to shoot an advertisement for designer jeans or men's cologne.

"Ian told me so much about you," Ray said, extending his hand.

Paul accepted it and replied with a forced smile, "Nice to meet you."

"You must be pretty special," Ray said. "To help Ian get his life together like that. A lot of us tried."

"He is," Ian said. His loving gaze barely registered with Paul, distracted as he was by Ray.

"You're welcome to come along with us," Ray said. "We'd love to have you."

"No thanks," Paul said. "You two should catch up. You guys have fun." It was the appropriate thing to say in the situation. Much more appropriate than what he was thinking, which was, *Keep your hands away from Ian, turn around slowly, get out of here, and never come back!*

"It was great to meet you," Ray said.

Ray was handsome, considerate, and he seemed to genuinely care about Ian's well-being. Paul hated everything about him. Ian kissed Paul quickly on the lips before he and Ray walked out the door.

All evening Paul sat staring without comprehension at the flickering television, flipping through channels, waiting for time to pass. At ten o'clock, he expected Ian to walk through the door. The minutes seemed like hours. By eleven, the waiting had become absolutely painful. By eleven thirty, he was angry and resentful that Ian was out having fun without giving Paul a single thought. He hadn't even called. Didn't he care at all? Around midnight, he started to entertain himself with masochistic fantasies of Ian's fair hands on Ray's dark skin, their lips exploring each other's. The more he was pained by the images, the more vividly he imagined them. By twelve thirty, they were tearing at each other's clothes, caressing each other's shirtless bodies, unzipping each other's jeans. He seethed with anger and betrayal over an infidelity that existed only in his mind.

Ray's car finally pulled up to the curb around one twenty-five. It lingered there for a few minutes with no one coming out. Paul imagined a good-night kiss, Ian running his hands through that thick dark hair, the two of them laughing at the old fool inside. When Ian emerged, Paul ran from the window and leaped onto the futon so he wouldn't be caught spying.

Ian opened the door slowly and tiptoed inside. "You're awake," he said. He skipped over to the futon, jumped onto the spot beside Paul, and threw his arms around him. "I thought you'd be in bed by now."

"Why? Just because it's almost two in the morning?"

"It's past your bedtime," Ian said with a little laugh. It was meant to be flirtatious, but Paul was in no mood for a comment on his age. For the effect it had on Paul, Ian might just as well have said, "You're a boring, dowdy old man with gray hair and love handles. I have no idea how I ever got involved with a fuddy-duddy like you. So I was out having wild, passionate sex with someone much hotter and more appropriate for me."

Ian kissed Paul on the cheek. "We had a really great time. We went and saw this band. Orange something. Orange Divinity? Orange Disaster? Something with 'orange' and the letter 'd.' They were pretty good. Mostly covers, but it was fun."

"I bet it was," Paul said with a sneer.

"What does that mean?"

"You could have called me. I thought you'd be back hours ago."

"I'm sorry. I didn't know you expected me to. You could have called me if you were worried. I had my cell with me."

"You didn't think it might bother me that you were out with another guy half the night?"

"No. You told me to go out with him. How was I supposed to know you'd get mad about it? It's not normal."

"What was I supposed to do all night?"

"We invited you. You said no. Why are you acting like this? It was your fucking idea for me to go out with a friend."

"Is that all he is?"

"God! Yes!" Ian got off the futon and started pacing back and forth with his hands on his hips.

"What kind of friends?"

"Friend-friends."

"You seem close."

"I haven't seen him in ages. I told you."

"Were you close?"

"What are you asking me?"

"You know what I'm asking you."

"What language do you want me to say this in? We're just friends."

"You never slept with him?"

Ian stopped pacing. He shook his head and sighed deeply. "We played around a couple of times, okay? Just for fun. It wasn't anything. It was ages ago."

"Played around? What is that? Do you have sex with all your friends?"

"Yeah. Instead of shaking hands. What is wrong with you?!"

"Why are you getting so mad at me?"

"Because you're being a jackass! What do you want me to do? Do you want me to stop being friends with Ray?"

"No," Paul said. It was the only answer he could possibly give to such a question, but it was a lie. The true answer was *Yes, I do*.

"Then what?"

"I just don't understand. If you can just 'play around' like that, how do I know if it means anything with me?"

"You don't know if it *means* anything? You don't know if it *means* anything? You know what? Fuck you!" Ian kicked the end table, knocking it over. Then he stormed into the bedroom.

Paul got up, set the table back in its place, and then followed Ian. When Ian saw Paul standing in the doorway, he threw a pillow at him. "Get away from me. Sleep on the futon," he said.

"Just calm down for a minute," Paul said, holding the pillow in front of him. "Let's talk about this."

Ian's hands were clenched into fists. "What do you think I'm doing here? You think I'm just sucking your dick for the free room and board?"

"Don't talk like that. Why would you say that? You know I don't think that."

"I do? How can I know that? You don't know if it *means* anything? All this time, you think I'm just playing around? How am I supposed to feel about that? You tell me."

"I don't know."

"You don't know. Great! That's just great!" Ian went back to pacing.

A minute went by like that, Ian fuming and pacing and Paul staring at an invisible spot on the bedspread. Finally, Paul said, "It's just… I'm not used to being with someone like you."

"Like me?" Ian turned to Paul with his arms folded across his chest. "What does that mean?"

"Don't say it that way," Paul said. "It's not bad. I mean, you're so beautiful."

Ian rolled his eyes. "What's your point?"

"I see the way people look at you. You could do anything with your life. The second you decide what you want to do. I look at someone like Ray, and I wonder what you're doing with me. He's your age. He's—God—insanely good-looking. And you can just go out and have fun without worrying about what anyone says about it. Why wouldn't you want that? Of course I worry. I can't give you any of that. You *should* have that. I mean, you *must* want that. And all the men. How can I not wonder where I fit into that? I'm afraid you… you must have had better than me. You must… want better than me."

Ian rubbed his forehead as though he were trying to smooth out his furrowed brow. "You told me you had faith in me. Do you remember that? When we first met? You hardly knew me then. Why don't you have faith in me now?"

"I do. I do have faith in you."

"Then show me," he pleaded. "Trust me a little bit. I'm not comparing you to anybody. I wouldn't be with you if I didn't want to be. If I was going to cheat on you, you think I'd do it in your face like that? Just because you're insecure about stuff doesn't mean you can treat me like I'm the slut."

Paul nodded. "I know."

"Do you? I don't think you do. You have to stop torturing yourself with the other-men bullshit." The words caught in his throat. "You have to stop torturing me too, because I don't know what to do anymore. You're always the one pushing me away, you know that? It's not me."

"I'm not pushing you away."

Ian sat down on the bed. "You don't think I get jealous? You know who I'm jealous of? I'm jealous of Sara."

Paul was shocked. "Sara's dead."

"I know," Ian said. "How can I compete with that? She's an angel. The minister and Saint Sara. And I know how petty that sounds. You're so proud of her. You're never going to feel that way about me."

"Hey." Paul sat down on the bed beside Ian. "You're wrong. You're completely wrong. I'm very proud. When I look at you, and how you've turned your life around, I'm so proud of you. I can't wait to see what you do next. I loved Sara. But *you're* my angel."

Ian sighed and lay down on the bed. Paul could see his anger had faded, but it had been replaced with something else, a quiet uncertainty. Ian gazed at the ceiling, lost in his own thoughts.

Paul put a hand on Ian's leg. "Do I really have to sleep on the futon?" he asked.

"No," Ian said with a deep sigh.

"I'm sorry," Paul whispered.

Ian didn't say a thing.

The Attachment

Every five hundred years, give or take a century, part of Mount Rainier collapses, releasing a mudflow into the valley below. The town of Orting, Washington, rests in that valley on a foundation of mud that was at the top of Rainier about five hundred fifty years ago. A destructive river of mud is, perhaps, overdue. The three thousand or so residents of the farm town below know that if the mountain collapsed, it would take less than an hour for the sludge to come down, burying everything in its path in twenty feet of mud traveling at thirty miles per hour.

About two weeks later, Paul was wandering through the church, looking for Ian. It was time to go home, and he was nowhere to be found. Paul finally discovered him in the large conference room. He was painting the molding and had lost track of time. He was completely splattered with white paint. It was in his hair, on his clothes and shoes, and smudged across his cheek.

"Did you get any on the walls at all?" Paul asked.

Without thinking, he reached out to Ian and, with his thumb, rubbed the paint from his cheek. He was still standing with his hand on Ian's face when he noticed the two figures standing in the doorway. Two members of the board had arrived early for their meeting. They were frozen in the doorway—staring.

The concept of gossip originated with the Old English word "godsibb," which is a bit like a "God sibling"—a person related in God. We human beings are, by nature, storytellers. Sharing a story binds us together. A secret story is even more effective; it defines who is "inside" enough to receive information. Gossip says, "I trust you with this information. We're on the same team."

Ian's theory that people were too wrapped up in their own lives to care about theirs would probably have been true under normal circumstances—were Paul not the minister. But he *was* the minister, the center of the community. He was a common point of reference, a natural focal point for community stories.

The story of Ian and Paul had everything: a church leader and a beautiful boy with a questionable past, the thrilling possibility of scandal, and the opportunity to increase one's moral standing by expressing outrage while simultaneously engaging in entertaining homoerotic fantasy. People loved a good mystery too. They could compare notes in a game of "are they or aren't they?" It was like looking for "Paul is dead" clues in Beatles records. There was no chance that the rumors were going to just go away.

The carefully crafted biography that Paul had been trying to write about himself had been wrenched from his control. Now the gossipers were the authors. They would decide the moral and meaning of Paul and Ian's story.

The members of the church wanted to know the nature of their relationship. Even if they got to the heart of that mystery—if they learned "the truth," what would they know? Only that the two of them had sex. Was that really the "nature of their relationship"? How could they ever know the "nature of their relationship"? That is something two people spend a lifetime trying to understand.

Why had God brought these two souls together? What divine force had allowed such an unlikely pair to meet and fall in love? What did it mean—to love? Why did Ian inspire Paul so? Could either of them have become what he was without the other? Of all the mysteries about Ian and Paul, whether or not they had sex was by far the least interesting.

The next morning Paul sat at his desk with a mug of coffee and fired up the computer. When the e-mail program had loaded, he clicked on the envelope icon and watched the messages download. He could read the subject lines as they did. "Free V1agra!," "Fund-Raising Committee Meeting Schedule," "A Special Offer from Kohl's," and then "Church Policy on Homosexuality."

Paul's chest tightened. It took a minute for the messages to finish downloading so he could click on the one he wanted to read. It seemed like an eternity. The e-mail, from Mike Davis, had a paper-clip icon indicating there was an attachment.

"Paul," the message said, "the board has decided to put together a sheet clarifying the church's policy on gay and lesbian issues. Could you please review this and give us your input?"

Attached were all the official church statements on homosexuality, cut and pasted together into one document. There was nothing new. It was the same mumbo jumbo about not discriminating but not encouraging, welcoming gay couples but not blessing them in marriage, welcoming gay individuals but not supporting gay organizations, and of course, the real reason the document had been sent—the passage about "avowed, practicing homosexuals" not being allowed in the ministry because it was "incompatible with Christian teaching."

The document had not been sent to Paul for his review or input. It was a warning.

Paul got up without reading the rest of his e-mail and walked around the church. He was thinking about the Worship Committee meeting scheduled for that evening. Once a month the committee, which was chaired by Mike's wife Janice, met at a member's house. This time they would be meeting at Paul's place. The thought of having Janice Davis and Ian together in his house suddenly filled him with dread. He had no idea what Ian might say. He didn't want to paint the picture of their domestic life. It was too late to cancel the meeting. Ian simply could not be there.

Paul wanted to raise the issue with Ian on the drive home from church, but he couldn't bring himself to do it. He was distracted throughout dinner, unable to find the right moment to ask him. Ian loaded the dishwasher, and Paul said nothing. Paul took aspirin. He paced. Finally, he could wait no longer. He had to bring it up now, before the ladies arrived.

Ian was sitting cross-legged on the floor, leaning over a music magazine. He was listening to his iPod, bopping his head and singing under his breath in a tuneless mumble.

"Ian."

He didn't look up.

Paul shouted, "Ian!"

"Yeah?" he answered a little too loudly. Paul pointed at his own ear. Ian pulled the right earbud out and let it dangle on his chest.

"Listen," Paul said. "I was thinking…. Could you turn that off a minute?"

Ian removed the bud from the other ear and put the player to the side.

"Listen," Paul started again. "I was thinking. The ladies from the Worship Committee are coming by in a little while."

"Yeah, I know," Ian said. "You told me."

"No, it's…." Paul scratched his forehead. "I was thinking that maybe… if you wouldn't mind… maybe you could go to the library or something."

Ian looked confused. "You need a book?"

"No… I just thought…."

"You're doing a lot of thinking."

"I just thought that maybe it would be better if you went somewhere else for a little while. Just during the meeting."

"Went somewhere else?"

"Just during the meeting."

Ian's face tightened, creating a line between his eyebrows. "Oh, just during the meeting," he said. "Not for my whole life."

"I knew you'd get upset," Paul said, kicking at a fuzz ball on the carpet with his toe.

"Then why did you ask?"

"Could you maybe stand up? It's weird talking to you down on the floor."

Ian stood up, put his hands on his hips, and glared. Somehow that was not a lot better.

"Just during the meeting," Paul said again.

"Are you going to be talking about something I'm not supposed to know about?" Ian asked. "Like, are you planning a surprise party for me?"

"No, it's just all the gossip lately…. I think…."

"Jesus Christ!" Ian started to pace. "Everyone knows I live here. It's not a secret."

"I know, but it's different seeing it."

"Seeing it? What are they going to see? Me sitting on the futon?"

Paul looked up at the ceiling. "You're being selfish."

"*I'm* being selfish? *I'm* being selfish? Oh my God!"

"Will you…. You know how important my ministry is to me. I just want…."

"I don't care about your ministry? I don't care what you want? You think this is fun for me? You think I like it when you introduce me to people like I'm your ward or something? Why do you think I put up with that? Because I don't care about your career? Because I don't care about you? When was the last time you stopped to think about what I want? When?"

"Okay, calm down. You're right. You're right. You're not selfish. I shouldn't have said that. It's my problem. But...." He looked at his watch. "Can't you help me out? Just today. We can fight about it later if you want."

"Is this my home? Is it? Or is it your house and you're just letting me stay here?"

"It's our home."

Ian grasped the air in front of him with half-closed fists, too upset to find the words for what he wanted to say.

"It's our home," Paul said again. "Don't make this a bigger thing than it is."

"You're ashamed to be seen in the same room with me. How could I possibly take that personally?"

Paul rubbed his temple. "I didn't say that. You're putting words in my mouth. Look, they're going to be here any minute. Can we finish this later?"

"You want me to hurry up and get my gay ass out of your Christian house?"

"Why do you have to say things like that?"

"Fine, Paul. Whatever. You're completely fucking heterosexual." Ian violently grabbed his iPod and magazine from the floor. "You got your wish. I'm out of here. But don't expect me to come back." He stormed out of the house, slamming the front door behind him.

Paul chased after him. "Ian!" he shouted from the porch. "Ian! Come back here. Ian!"

Ian disappeared around the corner.

When Paul turned to the right, he noticed four of the Worship Committee ladies had already arrived. They had just stepped out of Janice Davis's SUV and were in the driveway staring at him. Rella Peters stood with her mouth open, holding a tray of cookies in plastic wrap.

It was well after dark before Paul heard the latch turning in the front door. He picked up the remote control and turned off the television. Ian stepped through the door and tossed his keys onto the end table like he always did. The ear pieces from the music player dangled from his front jeans pocket. A cigarette dangled from the corner of his mouth. They looked at each other a moment, saying nothing.

Ian sat down on the futon next to Paul, took a long drag from the cigarette, and then crushed it out in an ashtray-saucer. Paul took a deep breath through his nose, trying to detect the scent of alcohol. He smelled nothing but cigarette smoke. Ian seemed to be sober. He looked drained and tired. Pensive, but not angry.

"How was the meeting?" Ian asked.

"It didn't go exactly the way I planned," Paul said with a sheepish half smile. "I'm sorry I was such an asshole."

"Yeah," Ian said.

Paul leaned forward and spoke to his knees. "Mike Davis sent me an e-mail today. He sent this document with the 'official church policy' on gays in the ministry. Said he wanted me to 'review' it. I knew what he meant. That's the reason I was worried with Janice here…. I just… I panicked. I should have… I don't know…."

"Why didn't you say that? I mean instead of just saying, 'Get out.' That would have been a little better. I mean, it would still have been kind of dickish, but at least I'd know why."

"I don't know."

"You don't tell me these things, and I'm supposed to just figure out why you're all weird on me. I'm not psychic."

"Where did you go?"

"I went to a bar."

"You…."

"No. I almost did. I ordered and everything. Whiskey, rocks. No one should have to deal with this shit sober. I don't know how people do it. But I just walked away. You have no idea…."

"I'm sorry." Paul reached over to run his fingers through Ian's hair. "I was afraid you weren't coming back."

"I was thinking," he said, leaning away from Paul's touch.

"About what?" Paul braced himself for the worst.

Ian took a deep breath. "What… what do you want?"

"I want you."

"No, I mean, what do you want? Is this just…." He sighed and furrowed his brow, trying to find his words.

Paul waited.

"Where do you think this is going? Do you think we'll be together in five years… or ten?"

"I want to."

He shook his head. "It doesn't seem like it."

"Why? Of course I do."

"So, I mean, are you going to keep telling people I'm a kid who's staying on your couch until he gets on his feet? Because you know that's not going to work forever."

"I know."

"Have you thought about it?"

"I've… I try not to."

"You have to think about it. It can't stay this way."

"The church has been my life for as long as I can remember. If they knew…."

Ian shook his head. "Everyone knows already."

"They don't know."

"You're kidding yourself. They know."

"They suspect, but they don't know."

"What's the difference?"

"They don't have to believe it if they don't want to. If I actually said it…."

"Yeah…." Ian nodded slowly, then reached over to Paul and touched his cheek. His expression reminded Paul of the sympathetic glances people had given him after Sara died.

"I'm sorry I made you feel bad… again," Paul said.

"Yeah," Ian said. "Me too."

TWO DAYS later, Mike Davis came to Paul's office without an appointment. He sat up straight in the chair in front of Paul's desk with his legs spread wide and his hands resting on his knees. His expression was accusatory.

"I need to talk to you about Ian Finnerty," he said.

Even though he was not surprised by the purpose of Mike's visit, Paul felt his heart skip a beat at the mention of Ian. "What about him?"

"This is a little bit awkward for me." Mike spoke slowly, choosing his words carefully. "People are concerned about your relationship with him."

People. What a joke. Mike was the one who was fueling all the rumors and discussion.

"They're concerned?" Paul asked in an even tone.

"No one has a problem with Ian," Mike said. "We all like him. But he *is* a young gay man, and you're spending a lot of time with him. You understand how that might look to people?"

"How does it look?"

"Suspicious."

"You're making this into something ugly. It isn't."

"This is serious, Paul. There are some people who are—" He paused to find the right words. "—deeply concerned about this. I've known you a long time. I want to give you the benefit of the doubt, but you have the kid living in your house. If it's not what it looks like—if there's a good reason, explain it to me."

Paul crossed his arms over his chest and narrowed his eyes. "I don't have to explain anything."

"Normally I'd agree with you, but you're the minister of this church. So it is our business. No one is accusing you of anything. We're just concerned with the appearance of impropriety."

"There's nothing inappropriate about it."

Mike leaned back in the chair. "Then my suggestion would be you help Ian find himself another place to live. People might stop talking about this."

Paul shook his head. "I'm not doing that."

"I'm trying to help you. I don't think you understand how serious this is."

"You don't think I do? You want to know what's inappropriate? This is inappropriate," he said, poking the desk top with his index finger. "You coming in here and telling me who I should be friends with and who can stay in my house."

"If there's nothing going on, what would it hurt for him to have his own place?"

"He's fine where he is."

Mike shook his head, and after a pause, said: "Paul, I'm just going to ask you this directly. Are you having a sexual relationship with Ian?"

It would have been the easiest thing in the world for Paul to lie. It might have changed everything, or at least bought him some time. But he didn't like lying. He preferred to avoid the truth.

"I can't believe you just asked me that." He stood up and gestured toward the door. "I think we're done here, Mike. Thanks for coming by and bringing this to my attention."

Mike shook his head again. He got up and walked to the door. Before he turned the knob, he looked back.

"I've been to your house, Paul," he said. "You don't have a guest room."

Moments after Mike left, Paul experienced a state that could hardly be called an emotion at all. It was the blinding tension of his fight-or-flight instinct kicking in. His stomach was tight, his nerves were raw, and he couldn't think. He had to get out of the church.

"I'm taking the rest of the day off," he called to Julie as he passed.

"What about Ian?" she asked.

"What about him?" Paul barked. He'd had enough of people asking him about Ian.

"How is he going to get home?"

Paul pinched the bridge of his nose. "Right," he sighed deeply. "Can you take him home?"

"Sure," Julie said.

A few hours later, Ian arrived back at the house to find Paul sitting on the futon with a mostly empty bottle of wine.

"Wine," Ian said.

"I thought I'd be done with it before you got home."

Ian picked up the bottle and eyed its contents. "You came pretty close. I've never seen you drink before."

"I didn't want to drink in front of you."

"Being drunk in front of me is okay, though, huh?" He was smiling when he said it. "This is an interesting turnaround."

"I'm sorry I left you at the church," Paul said. "I just had to get out of there."

"I know. Julie explained it to me."

"She did? How did she know?"

Ian shrugged. "She knows everything."

"She should mind her own business."

"She's just worried about you." Ian sat down next to Paul and put his arm around his shoulders. "Tell me what happened."

"It's starting," Paul said. "The board sent Mike Davis to confront me about my 'inappropriate relationship' with you."

"What did he say?"

"He said I should kick you out of the house."

"Maybe you should. Maybe I should get an apartment. I wouldn't have to stay there. I'd just have an address."

"You really want to spend money on that?"

"It might help you."

"I don't want you to do that. It's like going backwards. It's too late, anyway."

"You told him?"

"No, but I didn't exactly deny it."

Ian removed his arm from Paul's shoulder and looked down at his knees. "I've screwed everything up for you."

"It's not your fault."

"Things were fine for you before I came along."

"No, they weren't. They were just more… stable."

"What happens now?"

"I'm going to finish this bottle of wine." Paul put the bottle to his lips and drank the remaining wine directly from it.

Paul expected immediate repercussions from his discussion with Mike, but that is not how communities work. They operate at their own pace. It takes time for an issue to percolate and vibrate through the group until there is enough critical mass to address it. For the next few weeks, Paul and Ian lived in a state of purgatory. Paul could sense the growing current in the congregation—*what should we do about the problem with our minister?* He saw judgmental glances everywhere, even where they did not exist. He no longer felt the church belonged to him. His detractors owned it now, and they were only allowing him to stay and go through the motions for a trial period while they planned their next move. He still had to perform all his regular duties, hospital visits, social events, and Sunday services. He did them with a forced smile and an imitation of compassion because he could not focus.

Ian stopped attending Bible class. There were no more playful suggestions from Ian in the sanctuary. In fact, they hardly spoke to each other at all during the day. It wasn't something they had agreed to do; it was just something that happened. They both sensed they had to keep their distance. If you didn't know them and saw them pass each other in the hall, you would most likely assume they were old enemies based on their cold looks and their gruff "hellos." Paul ate his lunch in his office so as not to risk sitting by Ian in the lunchroom. Ian stayed out of the office as much as possible. The cheerful banter with Julie was gone.

Instead of waiting for Paul with his elbows on her desk, Ian would finish his work, sign out, and wait for him by the car, quietly smoking a cigarette.

The strain exhausted both of them. They would come home, complain about the atmosphere at the church, share any new gossip they might have overheard, and then collapse in front of the television for a couple of hours before falling asleep and waking up to face the church again.

The irony was that regardless of what anyone else might have thought, Paul felt his love for Ian was of a much purer form than his love for Sara. This was not to say that he had not loved Sara deeply or that his motives for marrying her had been anything but sincere. But his union with her had given him social standing. He had been a respectable married man, doing what a man of his age ought to do in society. He had always understood that, as a man, one day he would fall in love, marry, and support his family. He had married her at the right age, when he felt it was time. The story existed in his mind before he even met Sara. She was the one he had chosen to cast in the role.

Ian fit no narrative at all. He could offer Paul nothing in the world. Ian did not bring social standing. If anything, he could only erode it. Yet Paul loved anyway. Ian sparked his imagination and touched his soul. That was all he could offer. Wasn't that more pure and more sacred? It was a strange inversion of the way the world imagined it—the blessed union with Sara, the profane union with the young man.

The Meeting

Mount Rainier is a vestige of her former self. Some geologists believe that the peak once rose to 16,000 feet, nearly 2,000 feet higher than the current summit. It is a site of constant change, of destruction and revision. The mountain, the very symbol of strength and permanence, is in a state of constant change, crumbling, fracture, and cleavage. New crags and new shapes are cut with violent wrenching— perpetual re-creation. The peaks and ridges are transformed but remain awesome and sublime. "Mountain decay," wrote the nineteenth-century arts writer Richard St. John Tyrwhitt, "is a sculpture of beauty."

IAN WAS at Emily's desk, in the dark, chewing on the nail of his middle finger. Paul watched him from a few feet away, at Marlee's desk. He had a strong urge to hold Ian's hand but didn't dare. They were sitting with the lights off so that no one who walked past the office window could see them.

The board had specifically asked Paul not to attend the meeting, which would allow the members of the congregation to discuss their concerns about the minister and his alleged affair with the custodian. At the end of the meeting, they would be taking a vote as to whether or not Paul should remain in his position.

So many wanted to attend that they had decided to hold the meeting in the sanctuary. This gave Paul the opportunity to listen in via the speakers that piped the Sunday service into the office. Julie had agreed to turn the microphone on. So Ian and Paul sat in the darkened office, listening to the discussion like a pair of criminals.

"We're talking about firing Paul for something we suspect is happening, but do we have any proof of it? Has he actually said that he is involved with Ian?" It was a woman's voice that Paul couldn't quite place.

"He didn't say it was true. He just said he wouldn't answer the question." That one was definitely Mike Davis.

"Then we don't know for sure. It's just gossip."

"If there wasn't, don't you think he'd say so rather than saying it's nobody's business?"

"There might be reasons he would."

"Like what?"

"I don't know. Protecting Ian or something. There may be some reason we don't know about."

"Do we even know for sure that Ian is gay, or is that just a rumor?" asked a male voice.

Various voices replied, overlapping. "Oh yeah, he's gay. He's definitely gay."

Ian shrugged and shook his head.

"He definitely is. He said so himself. At the blood drive. He said he couldn't give because they don't let gays give blood." That had to be Margaret.

"Yeah, and then a few days later, Paul took his name off the sign-up list."

"Thanks, Emily," Paul muttered.

"That's pretty suspicious."

"But that's not proof of anything." Paul recognized Julie's voice instantly. "There could be all kinds of reasons for that."

"You really think there's another reason?" Mike said. "They live together, the two of them took their vacation at the same time. Why do you think that is?"

"I don't know, but I don't think we should assume anything."

Next came an unrecognized male voice: "Come on. Haven't you seen the way they look at each other? They're clearly gay."

"I saw them in the conference room one time. It looked like they'd been kissing."

"We were not," Paul argued with the unknown voice.

"How does someone look like they *have been* kissing?" Julie asked.

Ian laughed.

"What I think…. This question of being gay or not gay…. I don't think that it's a problem if Ian is gay, but I don't know if Paul should…. Isn't the question whether or not Paul is a good minister? Because I remember, you know, when we met for the Worship Committee…. Oh, that was the time that Ian ran out of the house wasn't it? See, it seemed like there was something going on there."

"Rella," Ian and Paul said in unison.

"I know Paul is fond of Ian, but I always assumed he felt protective of him, like a son. Just because you're close to someone gay doesn't necessarily mean you're gay too," said an older woman.

"But that's the most likely explanation, isn't it?" Mike said. "All the other reasons are kind of a stretch."

"I just want to say something," said a female voice. "So what if he is gay? My husband and I are new to the church, and we came because we liked the minister. We love his sermons, and he's been really welcoming and helpful to us. As far as I'm concerned, it doesn't matter if he is gay or straight or from Mars. He's the reason we came here, and we're going to keep coming."

Another female voice: "I'm not homophobic. I don't care what two consenting adults do in the privacy of their own home…."

What two consenting adults do in the privacy of their own home, Paul thought. Was someone really using that expression about him?

"But we're trying to grow our membership. We have to be realistic. If you'd heard that this church had a gay minister before you came, would you have gone somewhere else?"

"It wouldn't have made any difference to us."

"But do you really think that's typical? Are most people going to come to the church with the gay minister?"

"There might be some new people who would actually come because of it. Because we are open to diversity. I think young people might be attracted to that."

"We might draw a lot of gays, but what about the normal people? Won't they stay away?"

"Normal people," Ian muttered. Fortunately, someone in the room had the same reaction.

"Normal people?" she said.

"You know what I mean, the families with kids."

"At least they're discreet. They're not in your face about it."

"Discreet," Paul repeated. *What an awful word.*

"I'm with Jodi," said a male voice. "Paul performed our wedding ceremony and our daughter's baptism, and he was supportive when my wife's mother died. He's like part of the family. I'm going to support him. I can't believe after all he's given to this community we'd even talk about letting him go over this."

"Me too. If he wanted us to know, he'd tell us. Otherwise, it's none of our business."

"I'm sorry, but doesn't anyone else find this whole thing disgusting?" It was a man speaking. "It may not be PC these days, but it's not natural. We are talking about the minister of our church. How could anyone be in favor of keeping him?"

"I'm with you. The Bible says it's a sin. He's supposed to be the minister. Would we keep him if he committed another sin?"

"Like what? Not honoring his father and mother?"

"It's not just that he's gay. He's fooling around with a kid."

"Come on, Mike," Paul said. "Tell us what you think."

"Ian's an adult," Julie replied. "He's not underage."

"But how old is he? Twenty? Twenty-one?"

"I think he's twenty-five."

"How does that look? The minister and the twenty-five-year-old janitor?"

"If it were a twenty-five-year-old female housekeeper, we wouldn't even be talking about this."

"Hooray, Julie," Ian said.

"But it's not a female housekeeper, is it?" a new voice chimed in.

"Look, everyone likes Ian," Mike said, "but don't forget, the kid is an alcoholic too."

"He's a recovering alcoholic."

"What if he has a relapse? Alcoholics have relapses. Remember how he ended up here in the first place? Paul scraped him off the floor. Is someone going to have to go and bail the minister's boyfriend out of jail or something? Think about that."

"You know Ian," Julie said. "Do you think that's going to happen?"

"It could. But even if it didn't, don't you think it lowers the minister's stature just a little bit to have taken up with this pretty young guy...."

Ian winced, as he always did when someone used word "pretty" to describe him. Paul was beginning to understand his aversion for the word.

"Doesn't that paint the wrong kind of picture? It doesn't make him seem very serious."

Another male voice began to speak. Paul thought it might have belonged to Emily's boyfriend, Bob: "I just want to say, I don't think gay people should be discriminated against in any way. And intellectually, I don't have a problem with it. But the fact of the matter is, it bothers me. It's just the way I was raised. The idea of two men kissing makes my skin crawl. I'm not saying I'm proud of it, it's just a fact. And so when I see him up there preaching, I can't help thinking about it. I'm distracted by it. I should be thinking about Christ, and I'm thinking about men kissing. That's a problem for me. If he stays, I think I would have to find another church."

"And do you really want him around our kids?"

"Jesus Christ!" Ian said. He went back to chewing on his thumbnail.

"Come on, no one is accusing him of molesting children," Julie said. "Let's not even go there."

"But what kind of role model is he for our boys?" It was another new male voice. "Are we saying it's okay? This is just a perfectly fine lifestyle choice? That's not what I want to teach my children. They get enough of that on television. They don't need to see it in church on Sunday."

"I have a question," asked a woman. "Can we legally fire someone for being gay? I mean, I think that's something we have to take into consideration. We don't want to end up on the wrong end of a discrimination law suit."

"The official council book says a 'self-avowed practicing homosexual' cannot be a minister," Mike said. "So we'd be completely within our rights to fire him."

"Is he a self-avowed practicing homosexual? He hasn't said he was, has he?"

"Does that mean if he doesn't say anything he can stay as long as he likes? Like 'don't ask, don't tell'?"

"I'm just not comfortable voting the minister out when we have no real proof that this is even happening." That voice was definitely Stuart Briggs. "If I was certain, I'd agree he has to go, but I don't want to punish someone on the basis of gossip, and until he admits it, I am not going to assume it is true."

The debate continued for another hour, sometimes descending into heated arguments, personal attacks, and shouting. Some threatened to cancel their memberships if Paul stayed; others threatened to cancel if he was fired. Eventually Mike said, "I think we have all had an opportunity to express our opinions, and at this point we're just going over the same territory. I think we should take a short break and then come back and vote on this."

Paul sat hunched forward with his elbows on his knees. He felt as though he'd been pummeled repeatedly with a club. Ian was chewing on the nail of his index finger, and his legs bounced.

"I need to go out and have a cigarette," he said.

"You can't go out there now," Paul said. "They'll see you. Just wait a little longer."

Ian stood up and took a pack of cigarettes out of his pocket. He pulled one cigarette out and tapped it on the back of the pack, then put it in his mouth. He raised his eyebrows, then reached into his other pocket and produced a lighter.

"You can't smoke in the building," Paul said.

"Yeah," Ian said, flicking the lighter. "Arrest me." He lit the cigarette, took a long drag, blew out a trail of smoke, then walked over to the back office window, which overlooked the playground.

Paul thought he should say something, but he was too drained to think of what it could be. They waited in silence.

When the votes were all counted, 53 percent were in favor of keeping Paul as minister. He could stay, but it was a Pyrrhic victory. He knew things could never be the same again.

The Backpack and the Fly-Eating Plant

In summer, Mount Rainier is alive with color; glacier lilies, pink and white heather, red paintbrush, and white anemones compete for the attention of the senses. The naturalist John Muir called Rainier's Paradise Valley "the most extravagantly beautiful of all the alpine gardens I ever beheld in all my mountain-top wanderings." Lummi Indian legend has it that this beauty was stolen. Back when mountains were people, Mount Rainier deserted her husband, Mount Baker, and took all the flowers and fruits with her.

PAUL NEEDED to cling to Ian for comfort and protection. He was the only other person in the eye of the hurricane with him, and Paul had never felt as connected to a human being. He was sure Ian felt the same way. That night Ian caressed him with so much tenderness that Paul thought he was trying to summon his soul to his skin. In the sanctuary of Ian's embrace, Paul allowed all the stress, the worry and shame, to drift away. They fell asleep wrapped in each other's arms.

Paul woke up alone in the bed. This was unusual. Ian liked to sleep in as late as he could. Paul went into the bathroom, brushed his teeth, shaved, and then headed for the kitchen, where he expected to find Ian at the table, sitting in his briefs, eating a bowl of Lucky Charms. Before he could get to the kitchen, though, he spotted Ian sitting, fully clothed, on the futon. He was staring in the direction of the dark television, smoking a cigarette.

"There you are!" Paul grinned broadly, sat down beside Ian, and leaned in to kiss him. Ian turned away. That was when Paul noticed the green backpack lying on the floor. The fly-eating plant, which normally lived on the kitchen windowsill, was sitting on the end table.

"Are you going somewhere?" Paul asked.

Ian took a long drag on his cigarette, then crushed it out in the saucer-ashtray. "This is hard," he said.

Paul hadn't seen it coming. He was shocked and dismayed, and yet he understood exactly what was happening. "You're… leaving?"

Ian nodded. "Yeah."

"What did I do?"

"It's not you…. God, don't you hate that. 'It's not you.' I've never been the one to do this before. It sucks."

"It's not fun for me either," Paul said.

"Yeah." Ian grimaced. He gazed for a moment at the fly-eating plant, then turned back to Paul. "You remember you told me everyone gets a second chance? I need one. You heard them last night. I'm never going to be anything but the 'troubled kid' here. I'm not that person anymore. I want to start over where no one knows who I used to be."

"We can do that. We can start over together."

He shook his head. "You know who I was too."

"I don't care about that."

Ian rolled his eyes up to the ceiling and shook his head again. "You can't forget," he said. "You remind me all the time."

"Give me a chance. I know I get jealous, but I'm working on it."

"Maybe it's just that I can't forget that you saw me that way." Ian reached out to Paul and ran his fingers through the gray hair at his temples. "You really changed me, you know? When you met me, I never even thought I could wish for what I wanted. I didn't think it would ever be possible for someone like me. Now I'm wishing for what I want. But I realized I want more than this."

"What do you want? We can do it together."

"We can't. I want to start over. I don't want to be a charity case or somebody's dark secret."

"I'm not ashamed of you."

"You can't help it. It's just the situation. I mean, what were we thinking, you know? You're a Christian minister. I'll always be a problem for you."

Paul started to object, but Ian cut him off.

"You know it's true. And that's always going to be a problem for me."

"I can quit. I can do something else. We can go to Massachusetts like you wanted. Let's run away and get married."

Ian smiled, a wistful smile full of all the things he longed for and no longer believed he could have with Paul. "You can't just quit," he said. "Being a minister isn't just a job for you. It's who you are. I wish I had something like that. That's why I love you."

"If you love me, then why? Let me go with you."

"You'd end up resenting me for it. I've done enough damage to your life. If I go now, you can fix things at the church. Just tell them it was all a misunderstanding and you were trying to protect me. They'll believe it. You can have your old life back."

"Don't do this for me. That's not what I want. I don't want my old life back." Tears flowed down Paul's cheeks. He made no effort to stop them or brush them away. "I was dead inside when you came along. I don't want to feel that dead again."

"You brought me back to life too."

"When did you decide all this?"

"At the meeting."

"You decided last night, and you're leaving this morning? You didn't give me much of a chance."

"I decided yesterday, but I've been thinking about it for a while…. I'm really glad I met you. Sometimes… I think it's not always supposed to last forever, you know? But it was… well…." His face finished the sentence. It was a positive emotion that he didn't have the words to describe.

"So last night…. What was that, good-bye?"

"What would you have done if I'd told you then?"

Paul thought about it. "I'd have held you longer," he said.

"Yeah."

After a moment, Ian stood up and flung the backpack over his shoulder.

"Do you know where you're going?"

"I thought I'd go west. Maybe see the mountains."

"Do you have enough money?"

"I'll get by."

"Wait," Paul said. He picked up his wallet from the end table and unfolded it. It contained only thirty-one dollars in cash. He took the money out, folded it in half with his index finger, and handed it to Ian.

"I don't want your money."

"Take it. I'll worry. It's not a lot. If I knew you were leaving me, I'd have gone to the ATM."

Ian laughed as he tucked the money into his back pocket; then he sniffled and rubbed his nose.

"Keep my number," Paul said. "If you change your mind… even… even if you don't—if you get in trouble, anything. I'll always be here for you."

"You'll be fine, you know," Ian said as a tear escaped down his cheek. "You'll meet a beautiful woman. And you'll put her on a pedestal. Maybe she'll be able to live up to it."

Paul leaned into Ian. Ian reached up and wiped the tears from Paul's face and drew him in for a last, lingering kiss. As it faded, they held onto each other, each trying to memorize the feeling. Paul lowered his head. "Don't go," he whispered.

Ian backed away and picked up the fly-eating plant from the end table. He held it up for a moment for Paul to see. Then he turned and walked out the door.

Paul followed him and stood in the doorway, watching him walk to the end of the block, that familiar gait, head high, leading with his hips. Paul tried to memorize his movements. When Ian got to the corner, he turned around. For a moment Paul thought he had changed his mind, that he would come running back and throw himself into Paul's arms like a scene from a Hollywood romance. He didn't. They held a long look. Then Ian waved, turned the corner, and disappeared.

Paul didn't go into the church that day or the next day. Julie called and left messages on his voice mail, asking where they were, but he didn't call back. He couldn't face the questions, the gossip, or the spot in the office where he had sat with Ian just a day before, listening to the church members' meeting. By Thursday, though, he knew he had no choice.

"Where have you been?" Julie asked when she saw him. "I've been really worried. Are you okay? Where is Ian?"

"You should put out an ad for a new custodian."

"Why?"

"Can you send out an all-church e-mail for me?"

"Sure."

"Tell them that I'm going to make an important announcement on Sunday during the service."

"What is it?"

"I'd rather tell everybody at once."

"Paul, did you ask Ian to leave?"

"No," he said, and he went into his office. He had not even sat down at his desk when Julie knocked on the door. She entered without giving him a chance to tell her to go away.

"What's going on, Paul?"

Paul pressed his lips together. He wanted to answer without any emotion, but his body couldn't handle the strain. His voice cracked. "He left. We listened to everything they said at that meeting…. He's not coming back."

"Maybe I could try calling him and tell him we want him here."

"He's not at the house. He's gone. He left. I tried to call but he changed his cell phone number or something. I can't reach him. I don't know where he is."

"I'm sorry," she said.

All this time he'd thought he had to hide his love for Ian from her. Now he could see it in her face. She knew and had probably known for a long time. And it was okay. She understood, and she cared. She opened her arms, and he accepted the hug. She held him as long as he needed without letting go.

SUNDAY

In his 1864 book The Sacred Mountains, *a Presbyterian minister named Joel Tyler Headley wrote, "There are some mountains standing on this sphere of ours that seem almost conscious beings, and if they would but speak, and tell what they have seen and felt, the traveler who pauses at their base would tremble with awe and alarm.... Thus do mountain summits stand the silent yet most eloquent historians of heaven and earth... their solitude and far removal from human interruption and the sounds of busy life, render them better fitted for such communications than the plain and the city."*

THE CHURCH was packed that Sunday. The largest attendance the church had ever seen. Everyone knew about the outcome of the big vote and that Paul would be making a special announcement. It was the greatest drama in their church history, much more interesting than anything on TV. No one wanted to miss whatever was about to happen.

Congratulations, Mike, Paul thought. *You got your growth.*

Normally before service on Sunday, people talked and laughed. The foyer and pavilion were alive with voices. Those who spoke this Sunday did so in hushed tones. Few people greeted Paul when he passed. They were too uncomfortable.

Paul stood in the bathroom in his black robe. He took a long look at himself in the mirror. When he was ready, he ran his hands over the material to straighten out any wrinkles, took a deep breath, and walked down the hall and into the sanctuary. He could feel all eyes upon him.

Paul took his normal seat, and Emily began to play the prelude. There was all the regular ritual to get through before the much-anticipated sermon. The congregation sat through it with impatience. But Paul took his time. He performed the rituals with particular reverence. The reverence of someone who knows he is doing something cherished for the last time.

I would have held you longer....

When, at last, the time came for Paul to deliver his sermon, he stood at the podium without notes. He took a deep breath. There was no sound but the gentle rattle of the air conditioner.

"I won't be delivering a normal sermon today," he began. "This congregation has been through a difficult challenge. We're deeply divided, and I'm sorry. I'm sorry that I let this division happen. I probably could have put an end to it before it got to the point it did. But sometimes love can blind you. I love this community. I look out and I see adults who grew up here. I remember performing your baptisms. I see husbands and wives, and I remember performing your weddings. I remember the people who are no longer with us, and I remember performing their funerals. I am so grateful to every one of you for sharing so much love with me, for letting me be a part of your lives."

His throat tightened, and he took another breath and swallowed, trying to get his voice back.

"I want to thank all of you who voted to allow me to stay and serve as your minister. I'm humbled and grateful. And to those of you who voted the other way, I want you to know I have no hard feelings."

Paul looked down at the podium to the place where his notes would be if he had them. There was a long pause.

"I've been blessed to have two loves in my life. I don't know why God chose to send them to me. But I'm grateful. Each one taught me so much. And one thing I learned is that sometimes…." His throat caught again, and he continued at a higher pitch, "Sometimes when you love something, you have to let it go. As hard as that may be. And I love this church, and this community, too much to stay and see it torn apart."

Paul cleared his throat and straightened his shoulders. "That's why I'm resigning as your minister, effective this Friday. This will be my last service in this church."

There were sighs and gasps in the congregation. Julie, who was sitting in the front row, was crying. Paul's own tears started to flow.

"Thank you for the honor of allowing me to serve you for so long and for being such an important part of my life. Now it's time for this community to heal. Please join me in a silent prayer for healing."

Mountain

The first summit in the Bible, the first important peak, perhaps in human history, is Mount Ararat. It emerges from the floodwaters of an old world washed away, ready to accept a world reborn.

Paul wasn't particular when he scanned the job listings on the Internet. He wasn't seeking ministerial posts or professional jobs. He wanted something else. Something that would take him away from anything he'd done before. He lingered over listings for forest rangers and positions on fishing trawlers. He was waiting for something to jump out at him, a new world and a new life. No experience necessary. In the end it was one word that got him: mountain.

The ad for a Mount Rainier tour guide promised lodging in a pristine mountain setting. Paul let himself believe it was a direct sign from God. He would go the mountain, and he would find his angel there just waiting to be reunited. But there is a lot of west, and there are a lot of mountains. The reunion was not to be.

Paul took very little with him to Washington. He loaded up his car with his clothing and a few sentimental items, the pictures of Sara, the angel ornament, and Ian's favorite cereal bowl. The rest of the contents of his condo were sold by an estate agent. (He got about as much money for all of his worldly possessions as he'd originally paid for his big-screen TV.) He drove out of town past the church. As he took one last look at the building that had been at the center of his life for so long, he noticed the contractors on the roof. They were starting to repair the old steeple.

It was a Wednesday afternoon, usually a throwaway of a day. Tours were light in the middle of the week. But the weather that afternoon was ideal. The mountain was out, and the sky that surrounded its peak was an almost cloudless blue. The group was small enough for Paul to engage them each personally, to tell his most directly tailored stories. He could give them lots of time to wander and take photographs to bring home to flat states like Indiana and Kansas for the absent friends they wished were there to share the view.

Paul kept one special photograph in his bus. It hung from the rearview mirror, where it was always in his peripheral vision. As she got out of the bus for her solitary mountain time, a woman who appeared to be in her midthirties asked him about the picture.

"Is that your son?"

"His name is Ian," Paul replied.

"He's handsome. You must be very proud of him."

"I am," Paul said. "Very proud."

As the tourists made their way along the mountain paths, Paul sat at a picnic table quietly taking in the scene. He looked up, as he often did, to Rainier's awesome peak. It had become his church and his steeple. He thought about the steeple he had left behind, the clean white spire rising above a little church now run by a new minister. Did the new minister joke with Julie over lunch? Did he have to meditate before meetings with Rella? Did he embrace Mike's vision of growth, or did they clash? Did anyone place flowers by the modest stone in the churchyard that bore the name of Sara Tobit? Steeples, our man-made mountains, were always meant to outlast the people who built them.

Paul wondered if Ian had ever made it to his mountain. Had a snowcapped summit somewhere become Ian's steeple? Paul pictured him in the shadow of a peak, maybe in Colorado, awed by the majestic beauty. He imagined the indescribable beauty of sparkling pools and wildflowers in bloom reflected in Ian's blue-green eyes.

MOUNT RAINIER is a deadly volcano that will bury everything in its path. Yet the mountain is covered in life of all kinds: plants, animals, even species that exist nowhere else on earth. The snowcapped peak, the babbling brooks, the low clouds that hang over the valleys, the interconnected life. It takes your breath away. The seasonal wildflowers, the waterfalls, the patterns of moss—they're all here on loan. Nature is poised to destroy it all. When you forget that, Paul thought, you forget to cherish it. Maybe everyone should live in the shadow of a volcano. Maybe everyone does. What a shame it would be to stay away because you were afraid it would end. What a shame it would be to miss so much beauty.

LAURA LEE is the author of more than a dozen books on such topics as the science behind annoying things (The Pocket Encyclopedia of Aggravation), how weather changed the course of history (Blame it on the Rain), Elvis impersonation (the Elvis Impersonation Kit), and the joys of being broke (Broke is Beautiful), as well as one children's book, A Child's Introduction to Ballet.

The *San Francisco Chronicle* said, "Lee's dry, humorous tone makes her a charming companion… She has a penchant for wordplay that is irresistible."

She brings to her writing a unique background including stints as a morning show DJ, an improvisational comedian, a professional mime, a shopping mall Easter Bunny, and performing various odd tasks at folksinger Arlo Guthrie's office and nonprofit organization. She began her writing career at the age of twelve, when she published the article "My first Day of Junior High School."

Lee now divides her time between writing books, articles, and speeches, and producing classical ballet educational tours with her partner, the Russian ballet dancer Valery Lantratov.

Twitter: @LauraLeeAuthor
Tumblr: authorlauralee.tumblr.com/
Website: www.speechwriting.com/lauralee/
Blog: author-laura-lee.blogspot.com/
Goodreads: www.goodreads.com/author/show/18167.Laura_Lee

GNOMON

LUCHIA DERTIEN

www.dsppublications.com

www.dsppublications.com

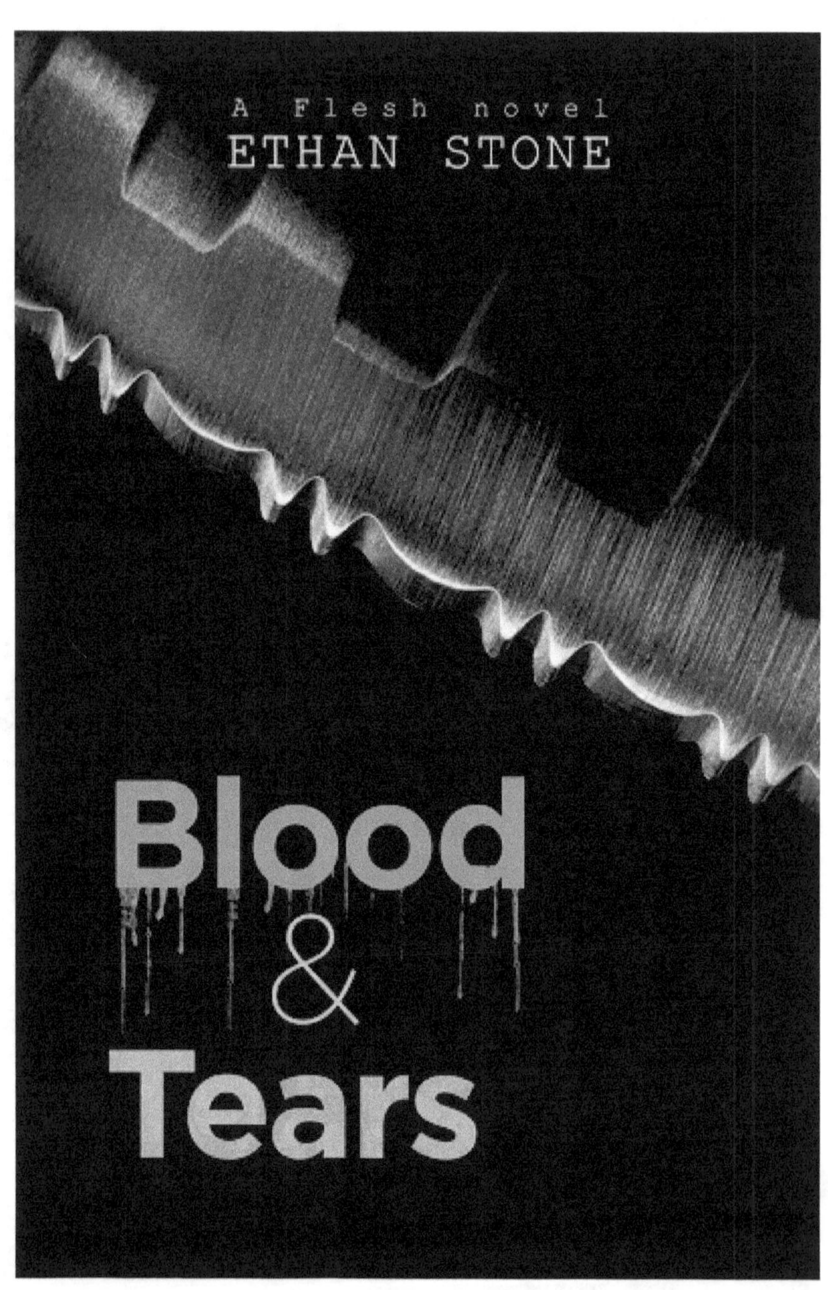

www.dsppublications.com

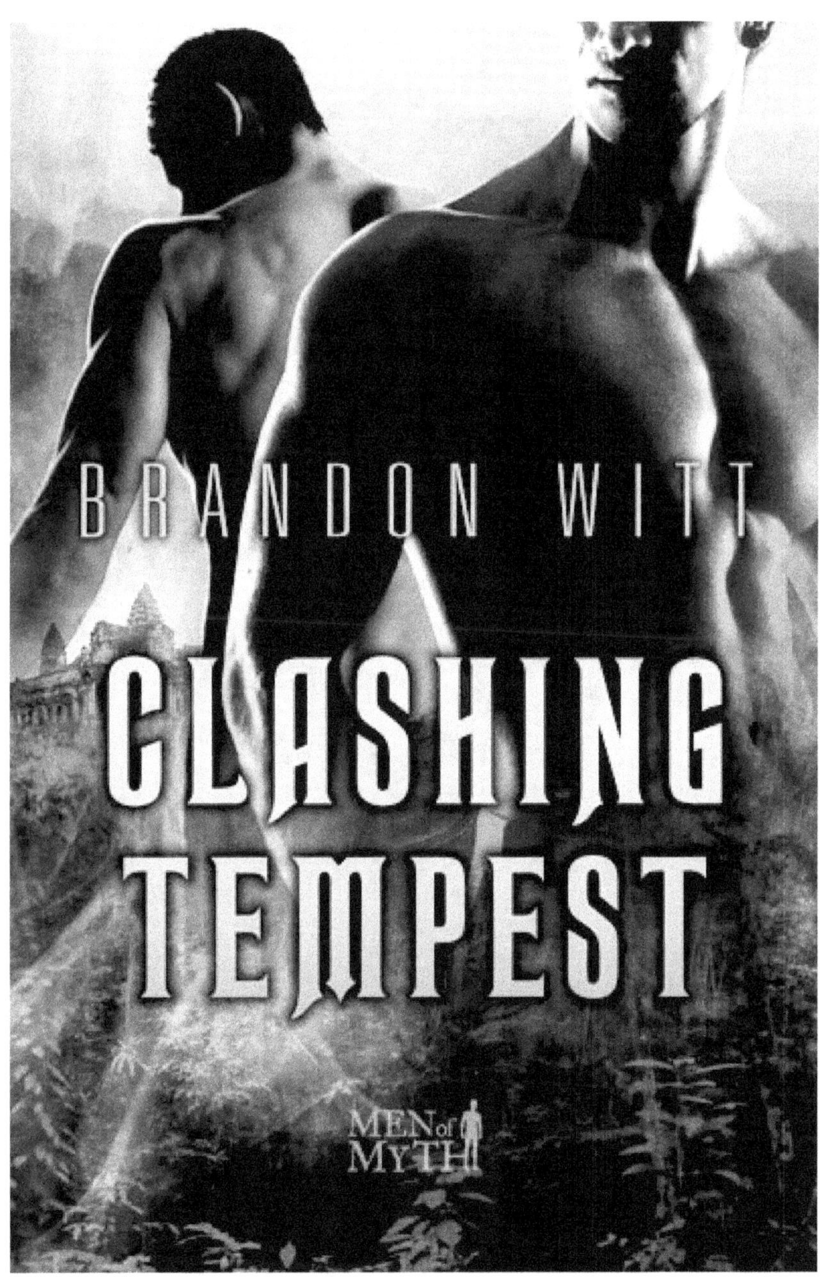

www.dsppublications.com

DSP PUBLICATIONS

visit us online.

WWW.DSPPUBLICATIONS.COM